The Boy
Who Invented
the Bubble Gun

Novels by
PAUL GALLICO

ADVENTURES OF HIRAM HOLLIDAY

THE SECRET FRONT · THE SNOW GOOSE

THE LONELY · THE ABANDONED

TRIAL BY TERROR · THE SMALL MIRACLE

THE FOOLISH IMMORTALS · SNOWFLAKE

LOVE OF SEVEN DOLLS · THOMASINA

MRS. 'ARRIS GOES TO PARIS

LUDMILA · TOO MANY GHOSTS

MRS. 'ARRIS GOES TO NEW YORK

SCRUFFY · CORONATION

LOVE, LET ME NOT HUNGER · THE HAND OF MARY CONSTABLE

MRS. 'ARRIS GOES TO PARLIAMENT

THE MAN WHO WAS MAGIC · THE POSEIDON ADVENTURE

THE ZOO GANG

General
FAREWELL TO SPORTS · GOLF IS A FRIENDLY GAME

LOU GEHRIG, PRIDE OF THE "YANKEES"

CONFESSIONS OF A STORY WRITER · THE STEADFAST MAN

THE HURRICANE STORY · THE SILENT MIAOW

FURTHER CONFESSIONS OF A STORY WRITER

THE GOLDEN PEOPLE · THE STORY OF "SILENT NIGHT"

THE REVEALING EYE, PERSONALITIES OF THE 1920's

For Children
THE DAY THE GUINEA-PIG TALKED

THE DAY JEAN-PIERRE WAS PIGNAPPED

THE DAY JEAN-PIERRE WENT ROUND THE WORLD

MANXMOUSE

PAUL GALLICO

The Boy Who Invented the Bubble Gun

AN ODYSSEY OF INNOCENCE

———————◆———————

Delacorte Press / New York

Copyright © 1974 by Paul Gallico and Mathemata Anstalt

Manufactured in the United States of America

First printing

Designed by Karen Gurwitz

Library of Congress Cataloging in Publication Data

Gallico, Paul, 1897–
    The boy who invented the bubble gun.
    I. Title.
PZ3.G13586Bo   [PS3513.A413]   813'.5'2   73-20287
ISBN 0-440-01789-0

TO
CASSIAN,
DAMIEN
AND
CARY

Nulla certior custodia innocentia.
—Horace

The Boy
Who Invented
the Bubble Gun

1

The miracles of the moon walk had
remained, in a sense, remote to Julian
as something taking place inside the
box of the big color television set and
reflected on the glass screen. The
visible, workable magic of the electric
eye that operated the entrance doors to
the San Diego Bus Terminal, however,
was something so differently enthralling
that it almost drove from Julian's head
the enormity of the expedition on
which he had embarked and which had
brought him to the terminal at half past
two in the morning.

Aged nine and a half and a scientist
himself, Julian was not unfamiliar with
the principle of the electric eye, but
encountering this phenomenon for the

first time in his life coupled wonderfully the mixture of the practical and the dreamworld that animated him.

He was carrying a small cardboard suitcase containing two changes of underwear and socks, a clean shirt, a toothbrush but no toothpaste, a hairbrush but no comb and, sealed in plastic containers or cellophane wrappings, the makings of tuna fish salad sandwiches.

The beauty of the functioning of the doors was that they turned Julian into a magician with powers over inert objects. He was startled and utterly enchanted the first time the portals swung open for him as he approached them. He passed through in a kind of daze and wonderment and they closed behind him. Even before the shock of noise from the busy bus station assailed him, he turned about, advanced, and the adjacent doors immediately made way for him and he found himself on the outside once more, the possessor of a new and captivating magical power.

Julian chose now to exercise it and changed himself from a small carroty-haired boy peering through steel-rimmed spectacles, clad in jeans, Keds, a T-shirt and a leather jacket, to a wizard in a tall conical hat and a blue robe spangled with silver stars. With the imaginary wand clutched in his fingers he gestured towards the entry doors, which obediently flew open.

Julian was about to enter once more, but now the scientific investigator, eternally in search of the truth, or whatever it was that made things go, came uppermost, and by discovering the source of the beam and edging gently backwards and forwards, he determined the exact spot where the doors could be kept open. This spot being rather central to the passage, people entering had to make their way around Julian, which certain parties in a hurry did rather testily, to the point where a slight disarrangement in the normal procedure of entrance to the waiting room caught the eye of a huge guardian armored in light blue, with the silver badge of a special policeman, who strolled over casually to inspect what was holding up the works. His shadow, or rather the aura of his leisurely and ponderous approach, fell upon Julian in sufficient time before his actual arrival to make the scientist-wizard realize that he was not there to explore the mysteries of the electric eye or the joys of supernatural powers. Instead he was on his way to Washington, D.C., to patent an invention, having stolen away from his home in the well-to-do Floral Heights section of San Diego, and from the sleeping household, with one hundred and fifty dollars in crisp bills in his pocket, constituting his grandmother's birthday present to him. He had no wish to be interrogated by any arm of the law. He was not frightened by the enormity of what he was doing; he was not in any sense running away from home. He was simply carrying out, or bringing to life, a dream that had become imperative. He had no desire to handicap himself. He therefore picked up his suitcase and trotted further inside the bus terminal where, having crossed its threshold, he immediately and irrevocably made an alteration in the lives of a number of people gathered there, some watching the electronic bulletin board of arrivals and departures. Moreover, Julian's crossing of this line of demarcation was to have repercussions affecting the two most powerful nations on the face of the globe.

But of this Julian was both too young and innocent to be aware. He could not know that every human action, literally almost every move made by people, acts upon the principle of the stone thrown into the still pond that initiates the ever widening circles that reach the shore.

He had never before been inside a bus station and the sounds and sights and the smells would ordinarily have terrified him had he not been armored by the importance of his mission. He had been a tinker ever since he could remember; every toy bestowed upon him he had taken apart and put together again. He had been a manufacturer of grandiose imaginings of wealth conferred upon him to reward his benefaction of mankind. Mechanically inclined, he had made things, but now for the first time he had invented something, an adaptation it was true, but nevertheless something which had never existed before. He had planned it, drawn it, machined some of the parts in the school shop, put them together, and it worked—well, except for one minor defect not essentially important. His schoolmates had seen it and coveted it. And his father had laughed at him.

The bus station is the crossroads of the masses too poor to travel by more luxurious means. It smells of them and the orange peels and banana skins and sticky candy wrappers with which they litter the floor and the fumes of the exhausts drifting in through the entrance and exit gates. They made their own music with the shuffling of their feet across stone floors, the shouts of children, the crying of babies against the antiphonal thunder from without of the engines of the big transcontinental vehicles and the overall metallic voices of the loudspeakers bawling information, directions and warnings to them unseen from on high like the voice of God.

Julian thus moved into this world where the neon tube turned night into day, where there appeared to be only a kind of shattering chaos of coming and going until as one moved into the midst of it one saw that it resolved itself, too, into long benches on which sat men and women with resigned, expressionless faces or nodding with half-closed eyes; and there was an information booth and a number of ticket offices and there were shops on the periphery—drugstores, newsstands, souvenir and candy stores.

Julian also saw people of his own age traveling, accompanied by grownups it was true, but nevertheless reassuring. On one bench, he noted, there was even a mother with a brood of seven, four boys and three girls ranging in age from about six to fourteen. They were surrounded by piles of luggage which the mother kept checking by counting on her fingers. She kept track of her family in the same manner, as one always seemed to be toddling or running off, to be called back shrilly and slapped. They fascinated Julian who had never seen anything like this before.

Julian moved through this now more ordered confusion to consult the electronic bulletin board which listed the Washington, D.C., departure for 3:10 A.M., but he wanted more verification and so he went to the information booth where two girls in uniform wearing caps with gold badges were looking bored and tired. One of them was manicuring her fingernails, the other was handing out a folder of some kind to a passenger.

Julian said, "I want to go to Washington."

The girl, without looking up from her manicuring, asked, "D.C.?"

"Yes, please."

The girl now looked up but saw nothing to interest her very greatly and said, "3:10 from Gate Sixteen. It'll be announced. The ticket office will open in about ten minutes. Over there." And she nodded with her head in the direction of a window that was unoccupied by a ticket seller. Thereupon she returned to her cuticle.

Julian noted the location of the window, spotted an empty space on a bench where he could keep it in view and went and sat down.

Sam Wilks was keeping a low profile. He sat off in a corner where he could watch the closed ticket window for the eastbound bus. He was unprepossessing looking and knew it. He had not shaved or washed or slept in a bed ever since he had fled from Carlsbad two days before. He doubted whether his description or what he had done had yet been broadcast or he would surely have been picked up. He was clad in worn Levis, a soiled shirt, leather jacket and a ten-gallon hat, sufficient of a uniform for that part of the country not to attract too much attention. And yet he had the kind of dark, surly and sour visage that the public had been educated to connect with the baddie and which led policemen almost automatically to stop him for interrogation. He knew what he wanted to do, must do, to break out of the trap into which he had got himself by killing a gas station attendant. He was aware of the blue-uniformed special policeman on duty in the terminal and, without seeming to be watching, always knew of the policeman's whereabouts. He was relieved that the officer did not seem to be looking for anyone and that there were no city cops about. Once on the bus, with a certain two articles concealed about his person, he would be alright, but in the meantime he did not want to be jostled by anyone. He sat chewing a toothpick, his pale eyes never still, planning and thinking hard about exactly what he would do.

Frank Marshall, with his square jaw, good brow, crisp curly brown hair and piercingly clear blue eyes, looked like a movie actor or the cartoonist's version of the All-American Boy except for the sardonic curl to his lips which, in repose, were the weakest part of his features. He was clad in khaki trousers, a checked shirt and a khaki garment which any Army man would have recognized as a one-time battle jacket except that all insignia—ribbons, rank, shoulder patches, collar badges—had been removed.

The twist to Marshall's mouth was partially self-mockery. He looked out upon the world with half-humorous derision. He was not bitter or bugged by what had happened to him, the violent alteration of his life. When he had returned from Vietnam fourteen months previously with something of a bankroll, he had been lucky in the crap games and he had thought it would be to pie in the sky, adulation, welcome and a job. Four months later had been when he had removed the insignia which proclaimed him, as he was finding out, not a hero but a sucker. Vietnam? Nobody wanted to know. He could not remove the scar that ran from his left wrist to above his elbow, gashed by a punji stick, but that did not show beneath his sleeve. As for jobs for veterans, that was a laugh. The West Coast was in a slump, his capital was depleted. Maybe he could do better in the East. He knew a couple of fellows in Washington. It was too late to go back to school. He was twenty-five. He needed a break or a stake of some kind.

With some time to kill, he sauntered over to the news-stand and thumbed over the supply of magazines and paperbacks.

A man by the name of Clyde Gresham was standing next to him watching him furtively out of the corners of his eyes. Gresham was soft. Softness was in every part of him. The shape of his mouth and rounded chin, the texture of his skin and the liquidity of the dark, moist eyes and the fondness that could come into their gaze. He was elegantly overdressed in loose summer clothes, negligee shirt with oversize collar and Givenchy tie, all in pastel colors to match a fawn lightweight suit. He carried his Panama hat to show thinning gray hair, silky in texture, brushed straight back from his forehead. His hands were beautifully manicured but pudgy and some-what shapeless.

When Marshall, fingering down an Agatha Christie from the rack, turned towards him, Gresham said with a warm smile, "Going far?"

Marshall examined Gresham fleetingly and got it in one. His cold eyes lingered on Gresham for no longer than another instant before he turned, without replying, made his purchase and walked away. Gresham remained standing there watching him go with a rather sad expression on his face.

The hands of the clock moved so slowly that Julian got up and wandered over to the coin-operated machine next to the drugstore, one of those movable cranes in a glass case with various valuable prizes embedded in a morass of jelly beans. The deposit of a coin activated the crane, which the player manipulated from without in hopes of getting the loose forks of the crane to latch onto a camera, radio or cigarette lighter. There were two people standing outside the drugstore not far from the machine and talking in whispers, a boy and a girl, but Julian paid them no mind. They were of high school age and hence inhabited an entirely different world from his. They stopped their whispering as Julian paused in front of the machine eyeing it. The push-in money slot called for a two-bit piece. Julian had some loose change in his pocket extracted from his tin box savings bank with the combination lock. Twenty-five cents was a stiff tariff, but the articles to be hooked were valuable and there was a camera that Julian immediately coveted.

He had his money already in his fingers when he examined the affair more closely and his inquiring mechanical mind looked it over and presented him almost at once with the sixty-four-dollar question. Why buried in all those jelly beans? Drag. Weight and surface. That was the catch against which the crane would have to pull. And all the prizes had either squared or rounded corners, nothing on which the forks of the crane could get a solid grip. Julian put the coin back into his pocket and turned away, grinning at the two high school students as he did so, but they did not smile back. When he had wandered back to his bench, the girl, whose name was Marge, whispered, "Oh, Bill, do you think he knew? I feel as though everybody is looking at us."

Bill said, "Aw, don't be silly. He was only a kid."

Marge said, "I know, but I can't help it. I'm frightened. I feel as though people could look right through me and know."

The boy was frightened too, but wasn't going to let on, or rather, he was nervous, worried and insecure, a virgin himself, as was she, about to explore the mystery which would make of him a man as all the others seemed to be.

Bill said, "Don't be scared, Marge. Look, I had an idea." He reached into his pocket and fished out a Woolworth's wedding ring. "I thought maybe you might—see, I got this. Here, put it on."

Marge took it and thrust it onto her finger. Bill said, "There you are. Nobody'll think anything now." She looked up into his face gratefully.

But they were not eloping. They were only slipping out of town to end the tensions that had developed through their liking one another and going together, but for them the step was more an act of conformation. All the other kids of their age group, the sixteen and seventeen year olds, had slept with someone or seemed to have, and talked and whispered and giggled in the locker rooms, putting up a kind of barrier that, under the constant sexual pressures of the times, seemed to have become unendurable.

Marge was plain in the sense that she was no startlingly

great beauty, but she had a sweetness of expression,
trusting eyes, gentleness and a downfall of fine, soft
chestnut hair. She was sixteen. Bill, a year older, was
loosely put together, tall, with the big hands and speed
that won him his position of wide end on the San Diego
High football team. The coach of the team was an old
square left over from his day in the bygone thirties who
preached that sex was weakening and therefore you kept
yourself and your energies for the game. Elsewhere Bill
was assailed by sex, sex, sex and a certain shame that at
his age he had not yet participated. Also, since he and
Marge both came from fairly well-to-do middle-class
homes, opportunity had been a problem. The adventure
upon which they were embarked was filled with excitement tempered by apprehension.

Back on his bench Julian watched the woman with the
brood of seven counting her luggage and her children
for the fifth time. The baggage checked but the kids were
one short, for she stopped at the sixth finger, looked
wildly about and yelled, "Johnny, where are you?" She
spotted him with his nose pressed to the window of the
candy shop. "Johnny, you come back here at once."

Johnny, a grubby boy of eleven, slouched sulkily back
to the fold. Julian wondered what it would be like to have
that many brothers and sisters. He had none.

A foreign-looking man, olive skinned, dark, with thick
black hair, passed by carrying an intriguing and extraordinarily shaped instrument case. Julian could only wonder what was inside it.

Next his attention was attracted to the man sitting

diagonally opposite him beside a fat and perspiring woman. A black flat briefcase obviously belonging to the man was between them and at this point Julian became witness to an international plot going awry. He had naturally no knowledge that the coming incident constituted a fiasco and, of course, no participation in it. The latter was only to come later.

The name of the man with the briefcase was John Sisson, a full colonel in the United States Army Ordnance temporarily attached to Military Intelligence in liaison with the CIA. He was clad in civilian clothes of lightweight seersucker which could not conceal his soldierly bearing. Tall, his short-cut hair graying, he had the stamp of authority and command. The lines about his eyes and firm mouth did not detract from what appeared to be a pleasant personality. One could not look at him without knowing that he was "somebody."

The drama got under way with the loudspeaker bawling, "Attention please. Calling Colonel Sisson. Colonel John Sisson, please. Will Colonel Sisson please come to the Dispatcher's Office. Repeat. Will Colonel Sisson please come to the Dispatcher's Office."

The Colonel waited until the repeat before he arose and hurried off in the direction where the terminal offices seemed to be. In his rush he forgot his briefcase, which remained on the bench where he had been sitting.

And now the action speeded up. A man whose false passport proclaimed him as being one Philip Barber, born in Waukegan, Illinois, and whose other equally false papers identified him as a plywood salesman, arose from behind a newspaper from whence he had been watching the Colonel. His real name was Nikolas Allon and he was a Russian spy connected with the KGB, a sleeper planted twelve years before in the United States for just this one moment. He was small, unobtrusive, nondescript with the toothbrush moustache of the traveling salesman, the type no one would look at twice, one of the faceless who pass by. He was moving not too quickly, not too slowly in a line towards the vacated bench, when the fat woman noticed the briefcase next to her and looked up at the back of the retreating Colonel. She arose, picked it up and hurried after him calling, "Mister, hey Mister, you forgot something." She was already ten feet away in pursuit of the Colonel when Nikolas Allon arrived where the Colonel had sat. To have picked up the abandoned article saying, "Sorry, I left my briefcase here," to have walked off with it, would have been one thing. To have initiated an incident now by snatching it from the fat woman and running was unthinkable in terms of the entire operation. Nikolas Allon just kept on going.

Julian watched the fat woman catch up with the Colonel and thought, "Haw! Grownups! Oh, boy, if I forgot my school satchel like that!"

The Colonel, checked momentarily by the fat woman's cries, hesitated, and was lost. Puffing and panting she caught him by the sleeve. "Mister, Mister, you forgot your briefcase."

The Colonel, since he came from Louisiana, turned and accepted it with Southern grace. "Why, thank you, ma'am. That's mighty thoughtful of you."

The fat woman toddled off. The Colonel, clutching his

briefcase, turned away. Nobody saw the black look of baffled rage come over his face or heard him grate to himself, "Goddamn effing busybody bitch!"

The episode over, Julian now reached into his pocket and pulled out a page torn from a popular science magazine, smoothed it out and examined briefly an article headlined ANYONE CAN PATENT AN INVENTION. Suddenly he became aware of a bustle and, looking up at the ticket window, saw that the ticket seller had arrived behind it and was arranging his gear preparatory to opening. There was a general surge in the direction of the window. Julian put away his article, got up, and made for it.

2

Julian had to detour, for the special policeman was on one of his rounds and heading in the direction of the newsstand on the other side of the terminal and, now that actual departure was becoming imminent, Julian was even more undesirous of attracting attention. When he reached the ticket window there was already a line, several of them people he had noted before.

The two high school kids were at its head and then the Colonel with his briefcase and the man with the toothbrush moustache, the dark foreigner with the strange instrument case and two unidentified passengers. Julian got behind them and back of him the queue lengthened, including

Frank Marshall, Clyde Gresham and a dozen or so others.

The ticket seller queried Marge and Bill, "Where to?"

Bill gave Marge a look of sudden panic, of which she was unaware. The phony wedding ring had given her confidence, but Bill, now faced with ultimate decision, had lost his cool. He was momentarily unable to reply.

The ticket seller said sarcastically, "Anytime. We got all morning."

Bill looked at Marge for help but only found an expression of trust as she said, "You say."

Bill gulped and made his decision. "Two. El Paso. Round trip." The ticket seller repeated the order, stamped and handed out the tickets. Bill paid.

Colonel Sisson appeared next at the window. He said, "Washington, one way, please."

The ticket seller droned, "Washington, one way."

As the Colonel put down his briefcase on the floor for a moment to reach for his wallet, Allon, directly behind him, twitched, momentarily so close to giving way to his impulse, that he broke into a cold sweat. He could have bent down, whipped up the case and been away in seconds, yet in time he realized that a hue and cry was not part of his assignment. At the ticket window he had recovered sufficiently, once the Colonel had departed, to say, "Washington, please. One way."

And then there occurred an incident which basically did not either surprise or discomfort Julian since he was used to grownups overwhelming or pushing kids about and accepted this as a fact of life. The cowpuncher in the filthy dungarees and stained jacket who suddenly ap-

peared out of nowhere and thrust himself in front of
Julian did not worry him except that the man smelled bad
and Julian was used to clean things. But what happened
immediately afterwards was strange and exciting.

Frank Marshall, three passengers back, saw the action
of Sam Wilks and it irritated him. He stepped out of line,
strolled forward, picked up Julian by the elbows and set
him down in front of Wilks.

Confused and bewildered by what was happening,
Julian looked up to see a young, tall, handsome man,
with the strangest, brightest blue eyes ever, confronting
the filthy, ugly-visaged cowboy. A veteran of television
conditioning, Julian knew that here it was, in real life, a
confrontation between a baddie and a goodie. What
would happen?

The goodie had the sweetest smile upon his face, behind which Julian was unable to read the slight hint of
derision and challenge, but there was no mistaking the
anger and truculence on the face of the baddie, though
Julian had no inkling of the man's rising gorge or how
dangerously near he was to a fatal explosion. But the
bulk of the special policeman now suddenly appeared
within corner-of-eye-sight and the fury went out of the
baddie's face, his lips mouthed something unheard and
he became utterly impassive and accepted what had happened.

The goodie said, "There you are, sonny. You're next,"
winked at Julian and went back to his own place in line.

The ticket seller, without looking up, intoned automatically, "Where to?"

Julian asked, "How much is it to W-W-Washington?"

Julian's stammer was another tribute to the overwhelming eminence and importance of his father, who,
as sales manager of the Dale Aircraft Company, president of the Rotary, and co-owner of the San Diego Bullets, the pro football team, was always holding meetings,
being interviewed and having his picture in the papers.

The ticket seller replied, "One way, one-oh-one thirty-
five, and round trip, one-ninety-two sixty. What'll it be?"

Julian said, "One way, please," and handed over six
brand new twenty-dollar bills.

The ticket seller snapped the bills into his cash drawer,
stamped the ticket and, with the change, shoved it onto
the counter and then, for the first time looking up, was
startled to see no one there. Or at least so it seemed for
an instant until he observed the top of Julian's head and
half of his bespectacled eyes just showing over the counter. Ordinarily this would not have worried him since
there was nothing in the table of organization of his
company that forbade selling a ticket to anyone who
could pay for it. But taken thus by surprise, he inquired,
"Say, sonny, you all by yourself?"

Julian felt a cold surge of panic. Was this then so soon
to be the end to the grand design? Adults lived by rules
and regulations and laws and things that were mostly
forbidden and one of them might be for a nine and a half,
almost ten, year old boy to travel unaccompanied.

The cowboy, the ill-smelling baddie, was standing,
shifting and shuffling impatiently, behind him. Julian
looked about and saw the special policeman, but he was
occupied talking to one of the pretty girls in the information booth, and then he caught sight of the mother with
the family.

Julian shook his head in negation and replied, "No, s-s-sir. Thank you." He took his ticket and change and, beneath the eyes of the ticket seller, wandered quietly over and joined the group of children.

The curiosity of the ticket seller was satisfied, besides which Sam Wilks was at the window saying impatiently, "El Paso, one way and shake it up, will you."

The ticket seller reacted to Wilks, "You've got all the time in the world, bud. Relax. El Paso, one way. Thirty-nine fifteen."

Julian wanted to talk to one of the boys and find out where they were going, but thought he had better not attract attention, at which point the mother went into her count again and when, having included Julian, she had reached the eighth finger, her countenance reflected such horror and incipient panic that Julian thought he had better go. He sauntered away, his last glimpse being of the woman at the finish of her recount and the look of relief on her face as she was able to stop at seven.

Marge and Bill were waiting beneath the electronic bulletin board for the bus to be called when Marge queried, "Why did you say El Paso, Bill?"

Bill replied, "I dunno. When he asked me I just couldn't think. I had to say something. But we can get off any place that looks nice. It'll be okay." Then, after a moment's hesitation, he asked, "What did you tell your mother?"

"I said I was staying with Dottie. You?"

Bill said, "I told 'em I was going fishing with Chuck and that we'd probably camp out."

All the old fears and doubts came back to Marge and she said, "What we're doing isn't right, is it?"

It was what Bill needed to bolster up his own failing courage—opposition. The female eternally changing. He said, "Gosh, Marge, I thought we talked all that out, didn't we? It's all different today. Nobody really cares what you do. We both want to, don't we? We both know each other. It isn't like we just met or anything."

Marge again was relieved to find what seemed like strength to her and whispered, "If you say so, Bill."

The electric sign on the bulletin board blinked their departure time and the loudspeaker, from on high, confirmed, "Bus three nine six for Tucson, El Paso, Dallas, Memphis, Nashville, Knoxville and Washington, D.C., immediate boarding Gate Sixteen."

Bill looked down upon the girl and felt stirred. He whispered, "Alright, Marge?"

"Alright, Bill."

The portals of Gate Sixteen now acted like the aperture of a vacuum cleaner sucking in passengers from various parts of the waiting room, twenty-nine assorted men, women, children, including the *dramatis personae* whose lives Julian was to alter.

The special policeman wandered over and stood casually by the gate. Sam Wilks was the first one through, one hand tucked inside his leather jacket. The next few seconds would tell one way or the other. But the Special now merely glanced at him, reflecting the disfavor he had registered earlier. He was obviously a cowpoke out of a job and on the bum. Wilks passed through the gate and removed his hand from inside his coat. Then his description had not yet been broadcast. But it might be at any moment. They would probably be looking for him at the border at Tijuana, but once on the bus he could still pull it off.

Allon had pushed to where he was right behind the Colonel and the Colonel knew it. Now it would be difficult for the Colonel to accomplish his mission. This sort of business was not his scene and he wondered and worried how he was to go about it.

Marge and Bill played the honeymoon couple to perfection. Bill had his arm about her waist and Marge glanced shyly down at the wedding ring.

Frank Marshall went through with a jaunty swing of his shoulders. So long, California, hello, Washington. Here comes Marshall.

Milo Balzare carried his instrument case hugged to his chest as though it were a baby.

Julian hung back. The special policeman and the gateman frightened him. What would happen when he produced his ticket? And always at the back of his head had been the worry that, sometimes as she did in the night, his mother might have gone into his room to see whether he was alright, found him missing and given the alarm. His fears were unrealized. The big fat cop smiled pleasantly at him, the gateman punched his ticket and as he had done already two dozen times, repeated, "Watch your step. All aboard, please."

The bus was clean and shiny and smelled of new car, plastic, metal and polish. Where one entered at the front door was a kind of a well with eight seats, four on each side behind the driver and looking out through the front windshield. From them there would be a wonderful view of rolling up the carpet of the road ahead, but because

Julian had not pushed to the fore, these seats were already taken. Then there were three steps up into the main body of the bus where the seats, two on each side, were divided by a central aisle and, of course, all the up front ones, too, were occupied. The baddie was in one of them in the very front row and Julian wrinkled his nose as he caught the odor. A few seats behind he recognized the man who had forgotten his briefcase. Julian had to keep on down the aisle to look for an empty seat. He came upon the young man, the goodie who had performed the strange action of protecting Julian's place in line. He was sitting on the aisle and Julian wished he might be next to him but the window seat already had a passenger. The goodie was absorbed in his paperback and didn't even notice him. But across from him there was an empty seat next to a man sitting by the window. The man was well dressed and looked clean.

Julian asked politely, "Can I sit here?"

Clyde Gresham turned to examine Julian. He said, "What? Why sure, sonny, make yourself at home. Here, how would you like to sit by the window so that you can look out?" He got up and stepped into the aisle so that Julian could squeeze past him. "Let me take your bag." He stowed it away as Julian settled into the window seat and Gresham occupied the other. His voice was filled with paternal oiliness as he asked, "There, how's that?"

Julian replied, "G-g-great. Thanks."

Gresham gave Julian a benevolent smile. "Not at all, not at all." He was unaware that the young man across the way had momentarily lowered the book in which he was engaged and was looking at him and that look was not exactly pleasant. Gresham was smiling down at Julian with the warm fondness of one who seemed to like children.

Looking towards the front of the bus, Julian saw a man in the uniform of a bus dispatcher appear to make a last-minute check of the passengers. The driver was already at his wheel. Julian suddenly thought, was he being looked for? Alarmed, he slouched down in his seat but the dispatcher's practiced eye had taken in the number of seats occupied, which tallied with the ticket count, and was satisfied. It was all over in a second and the only one who had noticed was Frank Marshall who had dropped his book again to steal another look at Clyde Gresham and had observed Julian's action, and he wondered. And after he had thought that there was nothing all that extraordinary in these times about a kid that age traveling by himself, he also thought that nobody ever got hurt minding his own business, and, returning to his book, let Miss Christie set her hook into him more firmly.

The dispatcher gave the driver the thumbs-up sign and left the bus, and the latter, working his lever, slid the hydraulic doors shut. He then picked up one of two microphones, the one communicating with the headquarters of the company, the other being for talking to his passengers, and speaking into it, said, "Three nine six, three nine six leaving San Diego on time. On time out of San Diego. Three ten A.M."

In the huge Dispatcher's Office of the bus company centered in Oklahoma City where a constant check was kept on all buses on the road, an operator heard the radio message in his earphones and spoke into his own chest microphone as he noted the time and the number on a pad, "Okay, three nine six. Take it away, Mike. Gimme a call from Yuma."

The bus driver returned his microphone to the hook, picked up the one for interior communication and said, "Okay, folks, settle back. We're off." He trod on his clutch, dropped smoothly into gear and moved his bus off into the night.

3

The bus passed through the business district of San Diego, thence out past the factories and finally into the dark countryside eerily lit by a waning moon, which threw its varying patterns of lights and shadows on the window through which Julian peered, still buoyed up by the excitement of his successful escape. The most difficult part, perhaps, of his project had been realized. There was no way for his family to stop him now.

Thinking back about them he saw them, curiously, as actors in an old-fashioned silent film moving jerkily and hysterically about in the wake of his defection.

If the impressions that parents

actually made upon their children could be fully expressed by them, adults would be appalled by not only the penetration, but the distortion. Size has a great deal to do with it plus the fact that a child's world knows no boundaries and may consist largely of fantasies and exaggerations.

There had been a spate of revivals of old-fashioned silent movies complete with piano and drum accompaniment the past few months on television, and the films had become a cult amongst the young. The interplay of light and shade upon the bus window turned it in Julian's mind into the picture tube. His imagination kindled rapidly and it was in those terms that Julian now reviewed the events leading up to his present situation. The dialogue he saw in the form of subtitles flashing across the screen.

The fact of the matter was that Aldrin West was overworked and overharassed by the demands of the era with insufficient time to devote to all his interests, as well as his family. Still, with all these handicaps he tried to be a reasonably good father. But that was not the way Julian saw it. Ellen West, his mother, tended to overreact and overprotect Julian, which completed his thoughts as to his family. He felt neglected by the one and smothered by the other.

The film began with Julian watching himself enter his father's study where Aldrin West was seen clad in striped trousers and cutaway coat at his desk heaped with papers, and speaking into two telephones at the same time. The striped trousers and cutaway, of course, were no part of West's wardrobe that Julian had ever seen but that was how important businessmen in the silent movies were always dressed. In the film Julian was clutching the diagram of his invention, and he now filled the bus window with the first speech title.

"DAD, CAN I SPEAK TO YOU?"

Even at his desk his father loomed large and menacingly over him. To children all grownups must be either friendly giants or ogres. Mr. West hung up the two receivers and glared at him. "WELL, WHAT DO YOU WANT?"

Julian held out his diagram. "LOOK, DAD, I HAVE INVENTED A BUBBLE GUN."

Julian's movie was going well and he showed some technical knowledge for he now saw a closeup of his father's face looking down angrily and laughing sarcastically. "HA HA. WHAT GOOD IS THAT?"

Julian cut in his own face in close up too. "I WILL MAKE A LOT OF MONEY WITH IT."

In the silents everyone seemed to move rather jerkily and there was no mistaking the emotions of a character, so Julian's father first clapped a hand to his brow and then tore his hair. "OH, FOR GODSSAKE, CAN'T YOU SEE I'M BUSY?"

In Julian's mind the piano and drum hotted up here. "BUT LOOK, DAD, I'M GOING TO MAKE A MILLION DOLLARS."

To a crashing of chords and a long drum roll Mr. West arose and pointed dramatically to the door. "WELL THEN, COME BACK WHEN YOU'VE GOT THE MILLION DOLLARS AND STOP BOTHERING ME NOW."

Crestfallen, Julian watched himself creep from the room. He also knew how and when to use a dissolve. He dissolved now to a title reading, JULIAN'S BEDROOM—MORNING.

He listened with satisfaction to the excitement music

(deedle deedle dum, deedle deedle dum, deedle, deedle, deedle, deedle, deedle deedle dum) as his mother entered in her dressing gown and then, as she saw the bed unslept in and the note pinned to the pillow, registered anguish, fright and despair. Julian was not quite certain how to get the latter across in addition to her waving her arms about and so he used a title, "SCREAM!"

As his pajamaed father rushed into the bedroom and his mother pointed to the note on the pillow, Julian reproduced it as best he could remember.

"Dear Mom, Don't worry about me. I've gone to sell my Bubble Gun invention. I will make a lot of money. Dad only laughed at me about it. I've taken the money Grandma gave me for my birthday and some underware. Love, Julian. P.S. Don't worry, I took some stuff for sandwishes."

His mother now pointed an accusing finger at his father. "YOU'VE DRIVEN OUR CHILD FROM HIS HOME."

"OH, NO I DIDN'T."

"OH, YES YOU DID."

"OH, NO I DIDN'T."

"OH, YES YOU DID."

His mother wrung her hands. Julian wasn't quite certain what that meant so he had her shake them as she moaned, "WHAT WILL HAPPEN TO HIM? HE WILL STARVE."

His father pointed at the note. "HE SAID HE TOOK SOME STUFF FOR SANDWICHES."

His mother flung herself upon the pillow. "JULIAN, JULIAN. OH MY GOD, HE'S JUST A BABY."

At this juncture Julian took some liberties with his estimate of his father's character and had him go soft. He went to his wife to comfort her. "NO, NO, MOTHER, DON'T

WORRY, HE IS A BRAVE BOY. HE WILL BE ALRIGHT. HOW I
HAVE MISJUDGED HIM!"

Julian closed off this scene nicely as his father and
mother fell sobbing into one another's arms and he used
another dissolve to: THE PATENT OFFICE, WASHINGTON.

He was standing there with several important-looking
men clad, of course, in morning coats except that they
also wore top hats. One of them unrolled a large scroll
decorated with seals and ribbons reading "PATENT FOR
BUBBLE GUN AWARDED TO JULIAN WEST," and with an inner
thrill, he read his final title, "THERE YOU ARE, MY BOY. THIS
WILL MAKE YOU A FORTUNE!"

Julian's technique told him that here was the moment
for THE END and to fade out.

Indeed they had left the environs of San Diego,
which remained only as a glow behind them, and were
pushing into the desert country where not a single light
was to be seen. The screen of Julian's window had gone
completely dark and the bus driver had switched off the
main illumination of the vehicle with only one or two
overhead reading lights still in operation. The enter-
tainment with which he had provided himself was over.
Julian grew sleepy and with a contented smile on his
face in recollection of the final scene he leaned back
and went to sleep.

They were driving dead east and the blinding yellow
rays of the morning sun slashing over the horizon caused
the bus driver to pull down the movable shade to protect
his eyes but, mounting, the sun smote through the center
of the bus and began to wake the passengers who stared
and lifted their heads groggily through the stuffy atmo-

sphere not yet cleared of the miasma from people who had been sleeping in their clothes.

The bus was making time on a straight, uncluttered road and was swaying slightly and Julian awoke to a moment of sheer terror of the unknown. Why wasn't he in his bed in his room in his home with his ancient teddy bear, from which most of the stuffing had departed, within reach, and all the familiar things in sight of eyes opened in the presence of another morning? He experienced a moment of overwhelming panic and loneliness as though a giant hand had plucked him from his home surroundings and flung him into some new and fearful dream.

Then he remembered and a little of his fright drained away from him. He was on his way to Washington to patent and market his invention, and show his father. To verify this he did not trouble to take in his surroundings but slapped the pocket of his jacket, which returned a comforting crackle, and then he put his hand inside and withdrew the paper, which he unfolded and studied lovingly for its verification of who he was and where he was and what he was doing.

There were two drawings. One of the exterior showing what looked like a compact, blunt-nosed, black metal automatic pistol. Indeed it was a replica of one sold in the toy shops and had originally squirted a stream of water when the trigger was pulled. The other drawing was of the internal mechanism, Julian's adaptation and invention, a gun that when the trigger was activated actually shot forth soap bubbles. Every one of the eight parts had been accurately numbered and labeled.

THE BUBBLE GUN

1. Soapy solution compartment.
2. Trigger-actuated soapy solution pump.
3. Soapy solution hose.
4. Bubble-making ring.
5. Soapy solution fill-up plug.
6. Rubber air bag.
7. Trigger-actuated air bag compressor.
8. Air nozzle.

OPERATION

Compressing the trigger, the soapy solution will be drawn to the bubble ring. The air bag will be compressed, releasing the air through the nozzle. This air will produce a bubble when going through the bubble-making ring.

In the lower-right-hand corner was printed, THE BUBBLE GUN, INVENTED BY JULIAN WEST, 137 EAST VIEW TERRACE, SAN DIEGO, CALIFORNIA, APRIL 25, 1973.

He regarded it lovingly, remembering just how he had done it, this combining of a water pistol and his soap bubble game. The rubber bulb of the air bag he had got out of the medicine chest at home, a game provided the ring that formed the soap bubbles at the muzzle, the tubing, too, had come from the medicine chest, but the spring, the compressors and the plungers he had designed and manufactured in his school shop.

He was still niggled by and slightly worried over its occasional crankiness in operation, when it would not function entirely correctly at odd moments, and he wondered again where he might have made a mistake or which part was responsible for the aberration. But, in point of fact, it even had its attraction when instead of the large bubble, a stream of smaller ones emerged for then you could go "Dah-dah-dah-dah-dah," and give a machine gun or wholly automatic effect.

And with a little thrill of remembered delight he thought back to the day when he had first shown it to the other children in his class and he heard again their impatient clamor.

"Hey, Julian, lemme shoot it."

"No, no, it's my turn."

"Aw, Julian, let me."

"He said I could next."

"Can you make me one, Julian?"

They had all wanted one. When he had got it patented every kid would want one and there were millions and millions. Then his father wouldn't laugh any more.

Now a voice said, "What have you got there, sonny?" And the effect was most astonishing. It was as though Julian had been living under some kind of a glass dome or that his ears had been plugged up and his eyes unseeing and now with this voice his ears were unplugged and his vision quite clear. He saw and heard everything, the arid landscape whizzing by, the whine and rumble and roar of the bus and all the passengers within, those he recognized as having seen before and those he did not, waking up, yawning, stretching, adjusting their clothing and chattering. He looked about and saw the grubby ten-gallon hat of the baddie where he sat up front and the short-cropped gray hair of the man who had forgotten his briefcase, the honeymoon couple not yet awake, their hands clasped and her head on his shoulder, the man with the strange instrument case and all of the rest of the passengers, black and white. Across the aisle the young man, the goodie who had taken his part over the intrusion of the baddie, still had his head thrown back in the sleeping position, but his eyes were open.

And the question, of course, had come from the man sitting next to him and, in the stuffy morning air of the bus, Julian was aware that this man exuded some pleasant kind of fragrance as though he used scented soap or some flowery toilet water.

Instinctively Julian's hand dropped over his diagram. He knew very well why the first thing he had to do was patent his invention. If you didn't patent it, someone could steal it. But he looked up at the man beside him and saw only the round, dimpled face and a pleasant smile which boded no evil intentions. He then replied, "My B-B-Bubble Gun," but he did not remove his hand.

Gresham said, "A Bubble Gun, eh? Well, well. What does it do?"

Julian replied, "It shoots bubbles."

Gresham's smile grew even sweeter and he leaned closer. "You don't say. Did you draw that?"

"Uh huh."

"What a clever little boy you must be."

Julian studied the man again and saw no further cause to distrust him. Besides which the praise had pleased him. He said, "I'm g-g-going to Washington to p-p-patent it."

Across the aisle this extraordinary statement from a small, stammering boy caused Frank Marshall to turn his head slightly to look and take in Julian and his scented companion, for his fragrance reached to Marshall and suddenly caused all his hackles to rise. He recognized the boy as the one who had been crowded out of line by that bum, but had thought at the time that he must surely be traveling with someone. Other fragments that had filtered through to his only half-attentive ears returned to his memory. What kind of a crazy deal was this, a kid going to Washington to patent a gun that shot bubbles? And where did this fat fag fit into all of this? It wasn't any of his business. Nevertheless he sat up and couldn't help sharpening his listening faculties.

Julian quietly folded up his diagram and returned it to his left-hand jacket pocket and then automatically patted the bulge of his right pocket.

Gresham asked, "What's your name, sonny?"

"Julian."

"Julian what?"

"Julian."

Gresham smiled indulgently. "I mean, what's your last name?"

Julian did not reply and simply remained silent, obeying the first pricking of the subconscious reflex of self-preservation. When his parents discovered he was gone they would undoubtedly call the police and if he, Julian, went around telling everybody his name they'd be able to find him.

His companion broke the silence by saying, "My name is Gresham; Clyde Gresham, but you can call me Clyde, eh Julian?"

Julian remained silent but across the aisle Marshall

shifted uneasily in response to the deep-seated instinct
of an animal alerting to something repulsive in another.

Gresham asked, "Where's your mommy?"

"Home."

"And your daddy?"

"Home."

"Where's home?"

Julian nodded with his head in the direction from
which they had come and said, "Back there," and then
added, "San Diego," though he thought the man ought
to have known since they had both got on the bus there.

"I see. Isn't anybody with you?"

Marshall could not resist looking across in time to see
Julian simply shake his head in negation while Gresham
asked, "You mean you're going all the way to Washington by yourself?"

Marshall watched Julian again nod his head in assent.
Gresham was bent towards Julian and had his back half
turned so that he was unaware of the light of mounting
anger in Marshall's eyes.

"My, you're quite a little man, aren't you? I must say!"

Gresham's voice was so full of admiration that Julian
looked up at him again and into the dimpled face with its
smooth skin and warm, friendly eyes. Praise and understanding from a grownup were rare things.

Gresham succeeded in keeping the tremor of excitement out of his voice. "Well, now, it just happens I'm
going a good part of the way. Would you like me to look
after you?"

Julian was enveloped by the bland smile and saw nothing to intimidate him. He was bright enough to realize

that all that lay ahead of him was unfamiliar and that
being "looked after" might have its uses, particularly
since there could be no question of this stranger having
any authority over him, and so he replied briefly,
"Okay."

"Splendid," said Gresham. "Then we're friends. You
see, I have no little boy of my own," and he slid an arm
about Julian's shoulder and gave it a squeeze.

Julian reacted to this as he did to all adults not of his
immediate family who seemed unable to be in contact
with children without wanting to touch them, pat them
on the head or take them onto their laps. He didn't like
it but then this was a part of the child's world, so that
when they did it he kept quiet and suffered it while making plans to get away as quickly as possible. These
thoughts led to an unconscious wriggle and Gresham
removed his arm.

The hard knot of anger forming inside Frank Marshall
had its physical reflection in the balling of his two hands
into hard, tight fists.

Looking out of the window Julian saw that the dun-
colored lonely country had given way to a few green
fields, some outlying barns, a railroad siding and then
clapboard houses and adobe dwellings indicating the
outskirts of a town.

The driver's voice came over the interior communication loudspeaker, "Folks, we're coming into Yuma,
Arizona. Thirty minutes stop. Anybody wants can get
some breakfast here."

The houses increased in numbers and soon the highway became the main street.

Gresham slid his arm about Julian's shoulder again and said, "You come along with me and we'll have a wash-up and some nice breakfast together."

Frank Marshall said a word between his teeth that made his neighbor look at him startled and wondering what had put the young man into such a fury.

Although he knew it was none of his business the intensity of the anger gathering within Marshall made him stir and struggle in his seat, stiffening the muscles of his shoulders and arms. So violent were his feelings that he was not able to remain there any longer. He got up and walked to the front of the bus and down the three steps to the driver's well where he stood close to the door as the bus drew up and came to a halt at the station.

4

Bill said to Marge, "We're coming into Yuma," and then looking at her questioningly. "Here?"

Marge had awakened with all the innocence and trust of a sleepy-eyed child. Her face had been burrowed into the hollow of the boy's neck and shoulder and his comforting arm had been about her, but now sitting up and suddenly in the midst of a town and feeling the bus slowing down and once more being asked for a decision, she felt the little panic waves that had beset her ever since she had left her home to go with him, and she searched for an excuse. A half of one was handy.

"Oh, dear, someone might know us. Myra, a girl in my class—we're sort of

friends—has an aunt in Yuma," and then it was her turn
to look inquiringly. "Are you sure you love me, Bill?"

The quick, glib answer refused to come to the boy's
lips. Love, love, love! Everybody was always yowling
about love. What did they mean by love? What was it, a
thought, a feeling, a stiffening of his member and the
urgent need to secure a release? Or was it thinking about
Marge when he ought to be doing his homework, or
watching the coach diagram a play on the blackboard and
suddenly remembering the texture of her hair, the pressure of her fingers on his hand, her proximity, the feel
and the smell of her clothes? He was happy and content
when he was near her but how could you tell whether
that was love? But if you said you loved someone, and
didn't, just to make them let you give them a feel, or
eventually go all the way, that was a rotten kind of a lie.
A curious kind of sense of justice had told him something
was unfair. In exchange for three spoken words a good
kid like Marge would give away everything she had. That
was all they wanted to hear but once you said it you
couldn't take it back.

He looked at Marge again and there was the physical
surge and, too, there was something in the slightly pa-
thetic curve of her lips, in the line of the young neck that
was moving and disturbing. If one looked too long one
might feel that tears could be dangerously close; un-
manly tears.

He said, "I dunno, Marge. I guess I must because
when I look at you it's as though I wanted to bust inside."

This satisfied her for she snuggled closer to him. But
it was Bill's own insecurity which led him to decision.

He said, "Maybe like you say, if Myra's aunt lives here she might be around, you know. We could have some breakfast and then go on maybe even as far as Tucson or Lordsburg. Nobody'd know us there."

The bus station at Yuma was classic, mingling the fumes of diesel exhaust with that of frying eggs and bacon. There was a lunch counter on one side, a newsstand on the other, a few benches and at the far end lavatories with large signs over the doors, MEN and WOMEN. There was also a small Indian trading post where a fat Navajo woman sold blankets, beads, basketwork and badly made turquoise jewelry.

Gresham apparently had had difficulty locating something in his luggage. He and Julian were by far the last to enter the waiting room and the majority of the passengers had already performed their morning necessities and were ordering breakfast at the counter or buying newspapers. Gresham, his arm still about Julian's shoulder, stopped to glance about him.

He said, "My, my, smell that bacon. And I'll bet they've got pancakes too. Would you like some pancakes?"

Julian said, "Uh huh, but I've got to . . ."

At the far end of the room two of the passengers emerged from the door marked MEN, one of them still adjusting his clothing.

"Sure," Gresham said, "we'll do that first," and with his arm increasing the pressure on Julian's shoulder they moved off in the direction of the lavatories.

Gresham had miscounted the number of male passengers visible in the waiting room by one. That one, Frank

Marshall, now stepped out from behind the corner of the newsstand where he had been waiting, and squarely into the path of Gresham and Julian, blocking the way. There was no longer any fury on Marshall's face. His expression was blank, bland, almost disinterested as he ignored Julian and in a quiet conversational tone said to Gresham, "Where do you think you're going?"

The shock and surprise to Gresham was total, particularly since there seemed to be nothing hostile in the attitude of the young man, who he remembered now had ignored him so pointedly back in San Diego. Only in the amazingly light blue eyes with which he was being contemplated did Gresham feel there was something disconcerting, a kind of stare which seemed to be taking all of him in and at the same time appeared not to be seeing him at all. Odd!

Gresham said, "What?"

In the same quiet tone, Marshall said, "Take your arm off that kid."

Gresham did not even realize that he had loosed his grip upon Julian as he said, "What? What do you mean? I don't get you. The little fellow has to . . ." He tried to make a move to circumvent the man blocking his path but somehow always found himself looking up into those freezing eyes.

Marshall said, "Get lost."

Gresham huffed, "Look here, what's the idea? Who do you think you are? I'm looking after this . . ."

Marshall's lips parted in a half smile, "You heard what I said. Split. Get out of here."

Released from the encircling arm, Julian moved a little

distance away, thus disassociating himself from the pair and whatever was to transpire between them, and he gazed with curiosity from the face of one to the other wondering what was going to take place. This was the second time that the man he had labeled as the goodie had intervened and played a part in things that were happening to him. Was Gresham a baddie, too? It had seemed as though he had only been trying to be nice. True, he had been a bit icky but then a lot of grown people were. What was it all about?

Here was a mystery. The two faces were close together, one handsome with its easy smile and the other suddenly disintegrating before Julian's eyes. And the boy became aware within himself of a feeling that he could not put either into word or thought. He only felt that it was one of mingled discomfort and relief.

Gresham made a last attempt. "Look here, you can't . . ."

This time Marshall made no reply whatsoever, nor did he raise his hand in any kind of menacing gesture. He simply stepped onto Gresham's foot, hard, and kept up the pressure as Gresham grimaced and howled with pain.

Marshall said sweetly, "Sorry, dearie," and then for the first time allowed a grating note into the softness of his speech. "You're off the bus, too. If I see you again you could really get hurt bad."

Julian felt a little frightened. Violence on the TV screen was fun. Men shooting, stabbing or battering one another, but right there, out in the open so close by, it gave one a curious kind of sickish feeling in one's throat and stomach.

Gresham knew he was finished. He pleaded, "Listen, I've got to get to Memphis."

Marshall said, "Sure, that's alright. There'll be another bus along. This is where we part company."

What a strange way to fight. Julian watched Clyde's round, smooth cheeks collapsing, tears gathering at the corners of his eyes, his lips trembling like a baby's, all the air let out of his figure.

Marshall knew that it was over and so he removed the pressure from Gresham's foot and stood to one side saying, "You're going to be a good boy, aren't you, sweetheart. You wouldn't want to end up the rest of your days a cripple, would you? Get going."

Gresham's nerve broke completely and without another word he turned and hurried away towards the exit from the bus station that led into the town, where he paused for a moment, anxiously looking back.

Whatever it was it was over and Julian was no longer frightened. If he felt a moment of pity for the stranger who had been destroyed before his eyes it evaporated into admiration for the man who had accomplished it with such ease and command and there was again a curious sense of relief as though some kind of a shadow of which he had not been aware had been lifted from him.

He asked, "What happened? Where did he go? Was there something wrong?" And then he had to give a little wriggle since for all of these novel excitements there was still the original morning need.

Marshall said, "Never mind. You got to go to the can?"

Julian wriggled again. "Uh huh."

Marshall said, "Alright, then get on with it," and he

nodded with his head in the direction of the men's room, but made no other move.

Once more looking up into Marshall's face Julian experienced a great glow of admiration underneath which was a strange feeling of satisfaction engendered by something so subtle that he was not even consciously aware of it, namely that Marshall had not offered to go with him.

He said, "Okay," and went in to the accompaniment of the sound of the automatic flushing urinals.

Marshall took out a bunch of keys that opened nothing he owned and led to nowhere he knew, and played catch with them for a moment before glancing over in the direction where Gresham was yet lingering. Marshall made a sudden absurd threat as though to throw the keys at Gresham who, at the menace, turned and hustled out the exit so hastily that his buttocks shook.

Marshall gave a half snort, half laugh, turned and waited for Julian to emerge from the men's room, apostrophizing himself as he did so. "Now, what the hell did you do that for? For chrissakes, Marshall, can't you learn to mind your own business? You could get stuck with the goddamn kid."

Julian emerged from the men's room.

Marshall asked, "Okay?"

Julian replied, "Okay."

Marshall said again, "Okay."

The first one had been a question, the second had been a reply and the third was a careless farewell with all that Marshall could put into it of satisfied insouciance as he sauntered off. He did not turn around to see whether

Julian was following him for that was the surest way with a stray of any kind to make him come after you. Julian stood there watching him go neither hurt nor puzzled over this ending to this curious incident. As he saw it, whatever it had been was over. Children are not apt to linger over events that are closed out or the never-to-be-understood behavior of adults.

He went over to the lunch counter and found an empty seat next to the dark-haired man with the strange-looking instrument case, consulted the menu and ordered pancakes with little pig sausages. When they appeared he doused them liberally with syrup and noticed that his neighbor had nothing before him but sat there rather unhappily hugging his instrument case.

Julian asked, "What's your name?"

"Milo Balzare. You?"

"Julian. What have you got in there?"

Balzare said, "A symphonia. For music. But it very old from other times."

"Can you play it?"

"Oh yes. Am coming here to America to learn your popping music." He looked hungrily at Julian's plate and asked, "How you say that please? I like."

Julian told him, "Pancakes and little pig sausages," and signaled the counterman. From Balzare it came out, "Poncakes and leetle pik sausage."

The counterman yelled through the kitchen hatch, "Toss one. Small porkers with."

The musician looked baffled, "That not what I say."

Julian giggled, "That's alright."

The order duly appeared. Balzare regarded the food

in amazement and said, "Is so difficult language. How you say—coffee?"

The counterman had just shouted again through the hatch, "Draw one," and a cup of coffee was served. Julian laughed happily. He was having a wonderful time.

Looking down the line Julian recognized passengers more easily now that many were there at breakfast. Far down towards the end was Marshall with coffee. He was looking straight ahead. Julian wondered whether Marshall might glance over and if he did Julian thought he might wave to the man, but Marshall didn't.

5

Boarding the bus after the morning
break in Yuma, Colonel Sisson
managed to stumble, drop his briefcase
and spill the contents all over the aisle.
Any film director worth his salt
watching this scene would have said,
"Oh for godssakes," and call for a
retake, but apparently none of the
passengers who were blocked behind
him while he scrambled to pick up his
papers, Allon, Marshall, Julian, Bill and
Marge and the black-haired musician,
thought there was anything
extraordinary in this and only casually
glanced at the papers, which seemed to
be mainly diagrams and blueprints. In
great and obvious embarrassment the
Colonel was making an attempt to cover

up the nature of these papers as he scrabbled them up off the floor and restored them to his briefcase.

While they waited the bus driver said to Marshall, "Where's the little fat guy who was going to Memphis?"

Marshall replied, "He ain't comin'. He changed his mind."

The bus driver shook his head in disgust. "He might have said something. Passengers!" The hydraulic doors hissed shut. He picked up his short-wave microphone, gave his call letters, listened to the dispatcher's voice for a moment and then said, "Three nine six on time out of Yuma." He then picked up the one for interior communications and said, "Okay, folks, we're off."

When the aisle had finally cleared and the passengers settled, Julian found that his strange friend had moved across and preempted his window seat. That left Julian a choice on either side of the aisle. He didn't resent losing his view. In fact he did not give it a second thought since it was quite in keeping with the hierarchy of his world as he had learned it. Children were there to be pushed around, but it did provide him with an opportunity to probe further into the mystery of the vanished Gresham.

He asked, "Can I sit next to you?"

Marshall looked up and noting Julian without enthusiasm, had in mind to say, "Why don't you sit over there?" And then realizing that he had taken the boy's seat, felt guilty and fell. "What? Oh, sure sure, go ahead."

Julian slid down into the seat. Marshall gave him his shoulder and looked out of the window as the bus pulled away from Yuma and hit the highway again. Julian waited until Marshall got bored with the scenery and made as if to turn for his book. Then he asked, "What's your name?"

Marshall thought, *Oh Christ. Well, I asked for it.* Aloud, he said, "Marshall."

Julian asked, "Marshall what?"

"Not Marshall What. Marshall. Frank Marshall. Okay?"

He looked to find his place in his book when Julian said, "Mr. Marshall?"

The man gave up. Okay, so he was going to have to cope with the kid. He said, "Just Marshall will do."

Julian then asked, "Why did you make that man go away?"

Marshall was aware that kids were a lot smarter and more hip than they used to be but he had the feeling that this boy had a peculiar kind of innocence and trust and probably would not have known what that son of a bitch was up to. He therefore produced that completely phony expression and voice used by adults when they are telling to their young a thumping lie which they are convinced will be believed.

He said, "Well, you see, kid, I recognized him. I've seen him before. He was a—pickpocket."

Julian clapped his hand to his jacket where the Bubble Gun design reposed. "Would he have picked my pocket?"

"Maybe he would have. He was a rat."

Julian said, "Why didn't you call the police?"

It stumped Marshall for a moment. This made his voice even phonier when he explained, "Well, now you see, sonny, that would have just held everything up and made a lot of trouble for everybody. And anyway, he didn't have his hand in anybody's pocket so I just scared the . . ." He pulled himself up in time. ". . . the pickpocket."

Julian considered this. Well maybe, but it didn't entirely make sense. Gresham hadn't looked at all like a pickpocket ought to. For an instant that same sense of dark foreboding which he had felt during that moment when Marshall had frightened Gresham away returned to Julian. Something else had been involved from which Marshall had protected him. His doubts caused him to look into Marshall's face half questioningly, to be greeted with the man's dazzling frank and open smile as Marshall said, "See?"

Julian reached into his pocket and produced the folded paper of his diagram and looking at it with satisfaction said, "He didn't get it, did he?"

Marshall was grimly aware of the double meaning as he replied, "That's right. He didn't get it." Then, indicating the paper, "What's that?"

Julian replied, "My invention. After I g-g-get a patent for it I'm g-g-going to make a lot of m-m-money with it."

The word "money" startled Marshall for a moment and a slight change of expression came over his countenance. He was about to reach for the paper but thought better of it. He said, "What are you talking about? Let's have a look at it."

Julian did not comply but said, "I g-g-got to work on it some more."

Marshall said carelessly, "Okay, so don't," which of

course produced an immediate unfolding of the sheet of paper revealing the diagram of the Bubble Gun. Glancing at it Marshall was surprised and even more surprised that he should be so. He studied it for a moment and then asked, "You did that?"

"Uh huh."

"What's wrong with it?"

Julian replied, "I dunno. Sometimes when you pull the trigger it shoots a lot of little b-b-bubbles instead of a b-b-big one. I've g-g-got to figure it out."

Marshall took the paper out of the boy's fingers and examined it more closely, including Julian's name and address at the bottom.

He said, "It looks alright to me," and then added, "Why don't you ask him?" and he nodded his head towards the front of the bus.

Julian asked, "Who?"

Marshall replied, "That guy up there. The one who spilled his papers all over the floor. I had a look at 'em. That was Ordnance."

"What's Ordnance?"

"Guns and stuff. He's probably Army in civvies. He could tell you."

"Do you think he would?"

"You could try." Marshall studied Julian for a moment with considerably more interest. "Where are your folks?"

Julian replied, "Home. In San Diego."

Marshall queried, "Do they know where you are?"

Julian shook his head in negation. ". . . but I left a note saying I was g-g-going."

Marshall's curiosity was driving him past the mild interest stage. He said, "It doesn't make sense. What's the plot, kid? Come on, give."

"My d-d-dad thinks I'm a sissy and no g-g-good. When I showed him my invention and said I was going to m-m-make a million dollars he laughed at me."

Marshall asked, "What do you mean, he laughed at you?"

"He said to stop bothering him and to come b-b-back after I had made my m-m-million dollars. That's why I'm g-g-going to Washington."

It was making less and less sense. A million dollars had a sweet ring in Marshall's ears but of course it was crazy. The whole thing was absurd. A kid going to Washington because his father had laughed at him.

He said to Julian, "You've got to be putting me on. What's with your old man? What does he do?" The printing on the diagram caught Marshall's eye again and he said suddenly, "Hey! West! Is your pop Aldrin West, the guy who owns the San Diego Bullets? Say, they're going to have a good team this year with Korvalski throwing the passes. I'll bet you're a real football freak."

Julian shook his head. "I'm not. It makes Dad mad. I think football's crazy."

Suddenly a vista opened for Marshall as though a curtain had been lifted. A kid that didn't like football. He said, "I get it. What do you like?"

Julian shrugged and said, "I dunno. M-m-making things."

Marshall glanced at the diagram more intently and then again at Julian. He said, "He must know you're gone. Your pop's probably having a fit right now. You say you left a note? Did you say where you were going?"

Julian said, "No. Anyway, he wouldn't care."

Marshall sat back for a moment and wondered just how true this was. These were such funny times that one couldn't believe half of what one heard.

But, of course, Aldrin West did care, his concern intensified by a feeling of guilt and further whipped up by one of his wife's few genuine hysterics at the thought of Julian, to whom she only referred as "my baby," somewhere loose in the United States—to the point where there had to be a doctor and sedatives.

The repercussion of all this soon reached into a corner of the Missing Persons Bureau of the San Diego Police Department where a bored sergeant in shirt sleeves put on a headset to take a call and poised a pencil to take notes.

He said, "Missing Persons Bureau, Sergeant Cassidy speaking . . . Who? . . . Oh, yes, Mr. West. Your address? . . . What's the trouble, Mr. West? . . . Did you say bubblegum? . . . Oh, a Bubble Gun. A gun? Has he got a license for it?"

West's voice nearly deafened him, "For chrissakes, Sergeant, will you listen."

"Sure, sure, Mr. West, I'm listening. You say he invented this Bubble Gun and left a note. Can you give me some details?" He repeated what he heard as he wrote, "Julian West, age nine and a half, reddish hair, wears glasses, has slight stammer . . . How was he dressed? . . . Oh, I see, you're not sure. And he didn't say where he was going?" He listened, wrote and repeated slowly, "Didn't . . . say . . . where . . . was . . . going . . . Okay, Mr. West, that shouldn't be too difficult. Kids usually hitchhike. We'll put it out on the radio. Some guy will pick it up in his car. I'll let you know as soon as we hear anything."

And a short while later the police teleprinter was tapping out the alarm for Julian: "MISSING FROM HOME, JULIAN WEST, AGE NINETEEN AND A HALF, RED HAIR, GLASSES, STAMMER. THOUGHT TO BE WEARING DENIM PANTS AND T-SHIRT WITH LEATHER JACKET. ANYONE SEEING PLEASE CONTACT LOCAL POLICE."

By mid-morning Bus 396 had metamorphosed from a transcontinental transporter to a cozy social center of passenger activity, relaxation and the usual familiarization. Two men, chess fiends, had already discovered one another by the thought transference that leads one player to find a second and were engrossed in what was to become a perpetual battle on a pocket set. They were already face to face, each with that gleam of fierce hatred in his eye that only a chess player knows for his opponent.

Four other passengers, two men and two women, had become involved in a gin rummy game, all strangers to one another. One of the women was a black, a large comfortable-looking person with the most deliciously rich laugh which rang through the bus each time she filled and laid down her hand. She always seemed to be filling and laying down and the others were not liking it.

There was so much going on to be seen and done that any fears Julian might have had at being off by himself vanished. The passenger across the aisle, a cadaverous, unhealthy-looking man with a long blue jaw, had a cup of water in his hand which he had obtained from the dispenser at the back of the bus and he popped a pill into it. His eyes nearly bulged from his head as the effervescence erupted from the cup in a foamy cloud which began to engulf the back of the neck and the hair of the lady sitting in front of him, who had a good deal to say about it.

Horror-stricken, the man was trying to explain. "Ma'am, I'm mighty sorry. See, I got to take one of these pills every hour, but it never done that before. It must be this here water."

Three seats to the rear the dark-haired musician whose name was Milo Balzare withdrew an odd-looking instrument from its case and began to tune it. Julian, of course, had to go and look at it. He asked, "Is that it—what you called it . . . ?"

Balzare replied, "Yes! This is hurdy-gurdy. Would you like me to play something?"

Julian said, "Yes, please."

The instrument had the neck, frets and strings and body of a mandolin except that at the bottom there was a curious kind of handle. Balzare began to turn this handle, which caused the thing to give forth a low humming drone against which he plucked out a gay little melody with a pick.

The character across the aisle said, "Say, that's great. Can you play any country music?"

"That was a little country dance—from the Auvergne," Balzare said, looking puzzled.

"Naw, you know, down-on-the-farm stuff."

Balzare said, "I do not know yet. I have come to this country to give concerts and to learn."

Marshall had put his book aside and had on his lap a small transistor radio, turned down, to which he was listening with interest. The broadcast was not audible in the general racket now going on in the bus.

Julian wandered away from the group that had gathered around the musician. He was hungry. He climbed up into his seat to enable himself to take down his suitcase from the rack.

Marshall said, "Watch yourself. What are you after?"

Julian said, "I'm hungry. Are you?"

Marshall said, "Not yet. I want to listen to the news."

Julian took his suitcase and strolled a few seats down the aisle and addressed himself to Marge and Bill who were holding hands. "Hello."

Marge quickly withdrew her hand from Bill's, sat up and smiled at Julian. "Hello. What's your name?"

"Julian. Are you two on your honeymoon?"

Here Marge almost gave the show away by repeating "Honeymoon!" as though the word were something poisonous before she realized that what with the ring on her finger it wasn't quite the right reaction and said, "Oh dear, how did you know?"

Julian said, "Aw, I've been watching you. Would you like a tuna fish sandwich?"

Marge exclaimed, "Would I!"

Bill was not too taken with Julian's presence. Small boys meant nuisance to him. He said, "Where are you gonna get a tuna fish sandwich from?"

Julian said, "Make it."

Bill looked surly. "Come on, who are you trying to kid? Why don't you beat it?"

Julian said, "I wasn't kidding. I'll make you one."

He knelt down in the aisle and opened his suitcase, displaying its contents, which also included a small, very dirty teddy bear with one ear missing and most of the stuffing out of it.

Curious now, Bill leaned over to have a look inside and was surprised to see a half loaf of white bread wrapped in cellophane, a plastic container of tuna fish, a smaller one of mayonnaise, some lettuce leaves in transparent wrapping, and a knife. With expertise from long-time practice Julian whipped up three tuna fish sandwiches, handing one each to Marge and Bill.

The latter had the grace to say, "Sorry, kid. You're great."

Julian said, "That's okay," reflected for a moment and then made a fourth which he took back to Marshall, saying as he handed it to him, "I'll bet you'd like this if you tried it." He sat down beside Marshall, his case beneath his feet, and chomped contentedly.

Marshall regarded him quizzically, bit into his sandwich and said, "Not bad. What else can you do?"

Julian had a mouthful at the time and so replied only with a shrug. He could also make a bang-up peanut butter, cream cheese and jelly sandwich if he had the ingredients.

Marshall ate silently, glancing every so often over at Julian. He had the air of a man with something on his mind.

When they were both close to their last bite and Julian

was licking his fingers, Marshall said, "Did you know the cops were after you?"

"W-w-what?"

Marshall indicated his now silent transistor set. "I just heard it after the news. General police alarm."

Wide-eyed with terror at what must surely mean the collapse of his grandiose dream, Julian asked, "Are you going to give me away?"

Marshall replied half truculently, "What do you think I am? Why should I?"

Julian glanced at the transistor. "Could everybody hear it?"

Marshall shook his head in negation. "Not unless they were listening. And what if they did?"

Julian said miserably, "I don't want them to catch me until I get my patent."

Marshall nodded, "Yeah, I got that. Keep your hair on. How old are you? The cops gummed it up as usual. I'd say maybe nine, nine and a half. That right?"

Julian nodded.

Marshall said, "Cheer up, the fuzz added ten years. The broadcast said a boy nineteen and a half years old was missing. They'll be looking for some jerk of a dropout. People don't like to get mixed up with the cops anyway." Casually, and only half meaning it, he added, "If anybody asks you, you can say you're my kid brother."

Relief, wonder and admiration glowed in Julian's eyes as he gazed up at Marshall. "Say, can I?"

Marshall suddenly realized what he had let himself in for. "Oh, for chrissakes, no," and then saw the hurt look of Julian at the rebuff and switched quickly, saying, "Alright, alright, so you're my kid brother."

Julian felt a sudden strange thrill in the vicinity of his breastbone, warm and satisfying, going on inside him and recognized it as something that occasionally happened to him when he was happy or pleased. He looked up at the man next to him and was comforted by the mantle of Marshall's protection and his last words repeated themselves delightfully in Julian's mind. *Alright, alright, so you're my kid brother.* An only child, Julian had often longed for a brother as a confidant. With a big brother such as this, one could dare anything. And now his scrutiny was beginning to yield some clues. Julian asked, "Were you in Vietnam?"

Marshall shook his head in negation and a curious expression came over his handsome face which Julian was unable to interpret. "What makes you think so?"

Marshall had removed his khaki jacket and it lay across his lap. Julian pointed to it.

Marshall grimaced and said, "Army and Navy Surplus Store. I bought it."

"Oh, no you didn't."

"What do you mean I didn't?"

Julian pointed to the battle jacket which now folded inside out showed Marshall's name followed by "sGT."

Marshall was irritated. Behind those spectacles the kid had eyes. He was going to be even more of a nuisance than Marshall had foreseen. "Smart guy, aren't you? Forget it, will ya, kid."

Julian was not going to be put off. If his new-found brother was going to turn out to be a hero he wanted to know about it. He asked, "What were you? Does s-g-t mean Sergeant?" He indicated the jacket once more. "You've taken off all the—"

Marshall turned upon him angrily. "Oh, for chrissakes, I said forget it, didn't I? That's ancient history. Couple of years ago. So I came out of school. So they grabbed me. So I went. So I came out. Any more questions?"

Julian was not too upset by this sudden attack for he had learned that words, even shouted ones, cannot hurt a child too much. If he had been born into a prior generation he might have chanted, "Sticks and stones can break my bones but words can never hurt me." Adults were recognized as being wasteful of words, repetitive and only half meaning what they spoke. And so he replied, "No, sir." And then immediately after inquired, "What are you doing n-n-now?"

Marshall was forced to repress a smile. Kids *were* funny and hard to beat. He replied, "What do you think? Looking for a score. Make me some bread."

Julian asked, "What d-d-do you do?"

Marshall laughed. "What do you want done? You name it. I'm lousy at it. If something's busted I can either fix it or fix it so nobody else can fix it."

Julian laughed politely at the old joke.

Marshall said, "Okay, now I'll ask you one. That was a lot of crap, wasn't it, about your old man? I mean him not caring about you?"

The question drew back a curtain and allowed Julian a glimpse which, in the flash of time in which a thought takes place, opened the whole vista of his life at home, part fact, part fantasy, and with this came the memory of his perpetual pain, sometimes only surface but mostly buried deep, in knowing that his father was disappointed in him. Julian quickly pulled the curtain shut again and merely shook his head in negation. It was not a lot of crap but what was the point in trying to tell.

6

In the San Diego Police Headquarters
and the office of a Lieutenant King, the
Sergeant who acted as his secretary was
holding a telephone receiver delicately
between thumb and forefinger. Enraged
sounds were emerging from it.

The Sergeant said, "You'd better
handle this, Lieutenant. And maybe you
ought to hold this thing with tongs.
Guy named West. He's boiling."

The Lieutenant picked up his
extension. "Lieutenant King speaking
. . . yes, yes . . . who? . . . Mr. West?
Aldrin West? . . . Yes, yes, sure Mr.
West, I know who you are . . . about
your boy . . . what? . . . Nineteen and a
half . . . but . . . hang on a sec, sir."

He covered the mouthpiece with a
palm and said, "Oh, brother, somebody

boobed! Phil, let's see those last alarms that went out. There ought to be one on the West kid."

The Sergeant shuffled through a sheaf of papers, and said, "Here it is. Runaway. The alarm went out this morning. Why? What's the matter?"

The Lieutenant took one glance at the sheet, murmured, "Oh Christ," and then spoke into the telephone, "I'm sorry, Mr. West, you're right. I'm afraid we've goofed. We'll send out a correction immediately . . . Yes, sir, we'll keep you informed. I'll be giving it my personal attention."

He hung up the receiver and said to the Sergeant, "That lame-brain Cassidy sent out the wrong age on that runaway West kid. Nineteen and a half. He's only nine and a half."

The Sergeant said, "It ain't Cassidy. It's that goddamn teleprinter. It's always doing that. It ought to be fixed."

The Lieutenant said testily, "I don't care who did what. Put out a correction and get it right."

Julian was happy. Traveling by bus was like finding oneself watching two movies simultaneously. There was the one flashing by endlessly outside the window and always changing and the other inside the bus, all the people and what they were doing, the music from the strange instrument and people visiting and making friends. The tires sang their whining song as they rolled through the wild, tumbled Arizona landscape, tortured into mesas, dry arroyos, sudden rock formations like cathedrals, and deep ravines. Marshall was deeply engrossed in his book.

Towards the front of the bus Fate, the eternal play-

wright, was preparing the first of the dramas it had decided to weave about the small boy with the red hair, the
steel spectacles and the stammer.

The plot, neatly worked out, surrounded the man with
the false passport who was Nikolas Allon, the Russian
KGB intelligence agent, and Colonel John Sisson. Allon
was worried and upset. The moment for which he had
been planted twelve years before in the United States to
assume a false identity had come. He had had his instructions and through a moment of bad luck which had led
to an attack of nerves he had failed. He had blown two
chances at the Colonel's briefcase and was certain that
there would not be a third and yet he dared not fail or
return to his superiors without some results. A change of
plan was called for.

The Colonel was equally frustrated. Everything that
had been so carefully worked out and set up, all his
instructions on how to carry the plan out, had gone
wrong. Unless he could improvise or in some way bring
about what was wanted he was in for a record-breaking
chewing-out back in Washington. He put his briefcase on
his lap, took out one of the blueprints therefrom, extracted a pencil from his pocket and for want of a better
idea at the moment, began to work over it, aware that he
was partly visible to Allon in the driver's central rear-
vision mirror.

The seat next to Colonel Sisson, who was by the window, was empty. So was the one in front, but the back cut
off the Colonel just below the shoulders. However, by
the movement of the Colonel's arm Allon was able to see
and reconstruct that he was working on one of the blueprints in which Allon was vitally interested. He therefore

prepared to put into operation a second gambit, the first having failed. To do this he had to reach up into the rack over his head, take down his small satchel, open it, search inside it and make certain preparations which took several minutes. This done he closed his satchel, replaced it in the rack and sat back to await his opportunity. In so doing he had missed the entrance of one of the principal, though wholly unexpected, members of the cast of the play. Julian had come strolling up the aisle and, standing by the empty seat next to Sisson, had queried timidly, "Sir, c-c-could I ask you something?"

Sisson, looking up and seeing an eager-faced small boy, had replied, "What? Oh sure, sonny, sit down."

As Julian did so, the Colonel quietly removed the diagram marked TOP SECRET on which he had been working and slipped it back into his briefcase.

Allon, glancing once more into the rear-vision mirror, saw only what he had seen before since the height of the seat covered Julian. The racket inside the bus effectively covered conversation. As far as Allon was concerned the Colonel was still doing exactly what he had been before.

The Colonel queried, "Now. What's on your mind?"

Julian said, "It's about my Bubble Gun invention, sir. Marshall said that you . . ."

"Your Bubble Gun invention?" The Colonel was startled because he had not expected to be tackled on a subject connected with his own department—hardware. And then he added, "Who is Marshall?"

Julian nodded with his head in the direction of the rear of the bus. "He's my—my friend back there. He said you'd know all about guns."

Again the Colonel was startled for his nerves were

not all they should have been. "Oh, he did, did he? How—?" Then, reflecting for a moment, he remembered the ruse of his papers scattered all over the floor. "Oh, yes, of course. Stupid of me. Well, what about your invention?"

Julian said, "S-s-something d-d-doesn't work right. Can I show it to you?" And he had the diagram half out of his pocket.

"Sure," said the Colonel. "Let's have a look." He took the drawing and spread it out upon the flat of his briefcase. In an instant his practiced eye took it in and a smile touched the corners of his mouth but it was not one of derision—rather, of interest with even a tinge of admiration.

He asked, "You dreamed this up all by yourself?"

"Y-y-yes sir, b-b-but there's a problem."

"What is it?" the Colonel asked. "Looks alright to me." And he examined the sheet more carefully as Julian explained and then the Colonel reached into his pocket for a pencil.

Allon stole another glimpse into the rear-vision mirror and the movements of the Colonel's shoulders and the angle of his head told him that his quarry was still working on a diagram.

Over the loudspeaker the bus driver announced, "We'll be in Tucson in twenty minutes, folks."

Allon had an accomplice in Tucson, another in El Paso and a third in Dallas, but the farther away the bus moved from the Mexican border the more difficult became the assignment. The time to move was now. He would have preferred the entire contents of the briefcase which were known to the KGB as details of a new type of weapon, but failing that, one clear picture of a diagram or blueprint of a significant part and the ordnance experts in the Russian army would be able to reconstruct the rest. The moment was at hand.

Too, conditions were right. The bus was barreling along at some sixty-five miles per hour on a not too perfect piece of roadbed that caused an occasional bump or sway. One would not be able to walk too easily down the aisle to the lavatory without clutching from time to time quite naturally at the sides of the seats to steady oneself.

The Russian interest in what the Colonel was carrying was such that they had been prepared to risk the hullabaloo that the stealing of the entire briefcase would set off. The other alternative was to secure a facsimile of one or more of the diagrams without the Americans being aware that this had been done. Allon knew that if he accomplished the latter now, there would certainly be a decoration ceremony at the Kremlin, possibly even the Order of Lenin.

And now that the time had come even his years of training could not overcome the onslaught of nerves that assailed him as he made his final preparations. Sweat poured from his armpits and began to bead his brow and most embarrassing was that it made the palms of his hands slippery. He wiped them dry carefully several times on a handkerchief.

At the rear of the bus Marshall had put his book down and had seen Julian speak to the Colonel and then seen him slip into the seat beside the man and he thought to himself, *Kids! They can get away with anything. They just go barging in and because they are young and innocent looking or have freckles or red hair they get away with it.* And then, with an inward smile, he wondered to himself what would be the reaction of an Army Ordnance bigshot when confronted with a gat that purported to shoot soap bubbles instead of bullets.

The smile died away as something niggled at Marshall. What the hell kind of Colonel was that who spilled blueprints and diagrams marked TOP SECRET all over the floor of a public conveyance? Memories of the past came crowding in rapidly before he could shut them out again but they remained long enough to remind him that the higher the rank, the greater the quota of imbeciles. He wondered how Julian would make out. If the Colonel was busy he would probably be sent packing.

From his viewpoint Marshall saw an unobtrusive little man several seats ahead of the Colonel get up and prepare for a march down the aisle of the swaying bus, or rather he did not really see but was merely aware of him for he was not interested in the movements of other passengers as he was in what the Colonel's reaction would be to Julian's diagram.

The Colonel was saying, "You invented that? Ingenious. And you say the problem is . . . wait a minute. I think it's a matter of the ratio of distance, isn't it?"

"Sir?" said Julian.

Colonel Sisson studied the diagram for a moment with intent concentration, and then, tracing with his pencil, said, "Well, see here now, take your figure six, the rubber air bag. You've got it too close to the muzzle, I'd say.

You've got your soapy solution hose okay and there'd be a buildup at the muzzle so when you first pull the trigger you might get some nice good-sized bubbles, but your connection from the rubber air bag and the air nozzle is too short for you to get a buildup for the next, so when you squeeze the trigger you'd be getting that whole stream of little ones," and then he added, "Did you ever try to make a working model?"

Julian nodded his head in assent and his hand stole to his right-hand pocket and yet he hesitated for if he had made a serious mistake with the gun he was ashamed to let the Colonel see it. But Sisson had not noticed, having become fascinated with the simplicity of the gadget. He sketched lightly over the diagram with his pencil, saying, "Move the rubber air bag back to here, shorten your trigger action and lengthen your air hose."

Stark with admiration Julian said, "Gee, sir, that's right. I ought to have thought of that." Then he added, "But if I d-d-did that, shouldn't I p-p-put another washer here?"

The Colonel said, "Good for you. *I* should have thought of that." And he drew the washer in and then added, "I guess you're a pretty bright kid. What did you say you were going to do with this?"

Julian was filled with exultation. "Get it p-p-patented, especially now that you fixed it. Gee, sir, thanks. You're g-g-great."

The bus favored Allon for just as he reached the vicinity of the Colonel it gave a violent lurch as the driver swerved to avoid a pothole and enabled the agent to let himself be thrown up against the seat. His quick eye registered the small boy next to the Colonel who was of no interest and at the same time gave him a split-second glimpse of the drawing on the Colonel's lap, that of an extraordinary and heretofore unknown piece of ordnance on which the Colonel was working with a pencil.

Even so the trained eye of the Intelligence operative was not as fast as was the Japanese mini-camera palmed in his right hand which practically fell about the Colonel's shoulder from the lurch and which took six pictures during the time Allon mumbled "Sorry," regained his balance and continued down the aisle.

Frank Marshall saw it all happening but it didn't register. Not even a minute splinter of light which seemed to flash from the unsteady passenger's hand and which might have been the reflection of a ring. Marshall's mind was on the amount of time the Colonel seemed to be giving to Julian. Wouldn't it be funny if there really was something to Julian's invention? If it worked, wouldn't every kid want one?

As the passenger came teetering along Marshall perforce looked up and saw that his color was a muddy green, he was sweating violently, his mouth was distorted and his right hand was tightly clenched as though in a spasm. He thought, *Oh Christ, the poor bastard's going to be sick. I hope he makes it.*

The Colonel studied the diagram a moment longer. How old could the kid be—nine, ten? He had been so engrossed in the simplicity and ingenuity of the invention that he had not even looked up when a shadow had fallen athwart it and somebody was apologizing for having stumbled against the seat. He had simply murmured,

"That's alright," and continued with his examination. He said, "There, that ought to fix it," and suddenly with a curious glance at Julian, "Look here, young fella, what about you? Are you really going to Washington to patent this?"

"Uh huh."

"What do you know about getting a patent?"

Julian fished forth the crumpled article from *Popular Mechanics.* The Colonel glanced through it. "Sure," he said, "the article's okay. Anybody *can* get a patent for an original invention, but you know, sonny, there's a lot more to it than this and it's not mentioned here." He tapped the paper. Then he added, "By the way, who are you traveling with? This fellow Marshall?"

Julian nodded, "Yes sir."

The Colonel suddenly felt bewildered and began to wish he had not become involved. He said, "I see," and then was compelled to ask, "And what about your parents? Do they know all about this caper?"

Julian again knew himself close to panic. Questions, questions, always questions. But he nodded his head.

Sisson said, "Well, and when you get to Washington? Have you got any money? Do you know anybody?"

The word "money" led to "grandmother" and birthday present. Grandmother would do.

Julian said, "My grandmother lives in Washington."

The Colonel snorted and said, "Your grandmother will be a great help in the Patent Office."

Subliminally Marshall was aware of Allon emerging from the lavatory too soon to have been ill and marching past him up the aisle quite steadily, his hand was no longer clenched, his color seemed to have returned. But what was far more interesting was that Julian and the Colonel were still actively chatting.

Marshall did not bother any more about Allon except to notice that the man was busying himself with taking his satchel down from the rack again and the bus was entering the outskirts of Tucson.

The Colonel handed back Julian's diagram which he folded up and began putting in his pocket. The Colonel said, "You know, this whole thing sounds cockeyed to me, young man, and I'm not sure I believe a word of it." But then he indicated the paper which Julian was stowing away and said, "However, I've seen a lot crazier ideas than this come off. The point is, your engineering is sound. Look here, if you need any help in Washington, get in touch." He produced a wallet from which he took a card with his name, rank, department and the telephone number of his office in the Pentagon Building. He initialed it and then handed it to Julian. "Keep this safe. You might need it."

After he had been overwhelmed with "Gee, thanks," and "Say, you're the greatest," and Julian had departed, he said to himself, *For sweet Jesus' sake, Sisson, why can't you mind your own business? What the hell did you have to do that for?* But he excused himself with, *Goddammit, the country needs kids like that.* His mind then turned back to the problem of his mission and the bad luck that had attended it so far. He glanced ahead to where Allon was sitting and could not think of a single solitary thing to do beyond going up to him, handing him the sheaf of blueprints with, "Here, your bosses would like to have a look at these." The next move would have to be up to Allon.

Julian had dropped into the aisle seat next to Marshall as the bus slowed down through the streets of Tucson. He said excitedly, "Say, he was great," and produced the diagram. "He showed me what to do. See here?" He took out a pencil of his own with an eraser, rubbed out certain lines on the diagram, traced over the Colonel's corrections and gazed with awe and delight upon the altered sheet. "B-b-boy, was I a dope. I should have s-s-seen that." Then, looking proudly at Marshall, "But the Colonel d-d-didn't see something that I s-s-saw, like here."

Marshall said, "Yeah," and then casually, "Did he say it would work?"

Julian said, "Sure, why wouldn't it? See, when I . . ."

Julian became aware that Marshall, who had been showing the most intense interest, was suddenly no longer listening to him and he looked up slightly bewildered to see that Marshall was gazing in a puzzled manner up towards the front of the bus.

Julian asked, "What are you looking at?"

Marshall replied, "Nothing. Never mind."

Nevertheless he continued to watch the actions of the little man who had looked as if he were going to be sick. He saw that Allon had removed his bag from the rack and there was a curious tension about Allon's neck and shoulders and all he could think of was a memory of a high school track meet, and the eight-eighty and the way the back of the competitor on his mark a few feet ahead of him had looked, all bunched up and ready to explode. And there was something else that he kept trying to remember that tugged at his mind.

Julian began, "The Colonel said . . ." but Marshall

swiftly put his hand on Julian's arm in a gesture that meant keep quiet and half rose out of his seat to see what Allon was up to. He was getting ready to leave the bus fast and Marshall remembered Allon had bought a ticket to Washington.

Then there was the bus driver's voice, "Tucson, Tucson, ten minutes, keep your seats please." The bus drew up to a stop at the bus station. The doors hissed open and several new passengers boarded.

At this moment the subliminal, that same which so often had saved that other Marshall and helped him during certain dangerous days to avoid the trip wires hidden underfoot, grenades hung from trees, pressure mines that tore one's legs and genitals to bloody shreds, the poisoned punji sticks buried in the ground and all the other booby traps, came startlingly to life and brought what had happened into focus. And even as Allon nipped out of the seat, out of the bus and was off running, with Colonel Sisson standing and looking at him in confusion, Marshall was down the aisle saying to Sisson, "Sir, excuse me, I may be wrong but I think that little guy that just got off took a picture."

Sisson said, "What? Picture of what?" He couldn't remember Allon's movements.

Marshall was saying, "Over your shoulder. When the bus was swaying. He almost fell over you. I thought I saw something in his hand."

Cold fear settled in the Colonel's stomach. He glanced at his briefcase, then gripped Marshall's arm, "Christ! When? Did you notice when he got the picture?"

Marshall said, "When you were talking to the kid."

The Colonel yelled "Son of a bitch!" so loudly that it startled everyone in the vicinity but particularly the man named Wilks occupying the front seat. Beyond the offense of his appearance, his behavior had been subdued ever since he had got on the bus; he hardly moved at all as though concerned with not attracting attention and did not get out during stopovers. He sat hunched by the window, hat pulled down over his eyes, moodily observing the scenery as it flashed by. Occasionally he pulled a road map from a pocket and studied it. The seat next to him was unoccupied. Two passengers had tried it, a man and a woman, and been driven away by his unwashed fetor. These defections did not seem to upset or worry the man.

But now as the Colonel rushed past him and out through the still-open door while reaching inside his jacket for his shoulder holster, Wilks immediately arose, his hand moving in an exact duplicate to that of the Colonel.

Marshall bumped Wilks as he dashed after the Colonel and momentarily distracted him from completing his draw. Wilks remembered Marshall from the episode in the bus station and the irritation gave him pause just long enough to see that the sudden furor had nothing to do with him. He removed his hand from his clothing, shoved his hat onto the back of his head and mopped his brow. He sank back into his seat and watched through the window.

Colonel Sisson and Marshall were just in time to see Allon at a little distance giving a taxi driver instructions. The Colonel produced his gun, a black Army .45. The bulk of the passengers in the bus were unaware of the curious drama being played out at the entrance to the bus station since Sisson had his back to them and they could not see the automatic.

There was a moment of frozen tableau like the stopping of a motion picture film on one frame as Allon, for one terror-stricken instant, his face a mask of fright, glanced over at the Colonel, the gun and Marshall. Then he nipped into the cab, slammed the door and was gone.

Marshall was unable to keep a slight tinge of contempt from his voice as he said, "You could have had him, sir."

For the first time Sisson took in Marshall wholly, and recognizing an ex-soldier, the Colonel reholstered his gun and said, "Thanks, but maybe I didn't want him with holes in him," and then he said, "Oh, goddammit, the stupid bastard." And suddenly he felt as though he was nine years old like the kid with that design and wanted to cry from sheer helpless frustration. "What a son-of-a-bitching foul-up!" For a moment, almost stupidly he regarded his briefcase and then said bitterly, "They'll have my chicken feathers for this. That crazy kid! Tell the bus driver I'm not coming back."

Marshall said, "I don't get it," but Sisson was already running for a second taxi, exchanged a few words with the driver, was in and gone.

As Marshall climbed back into the bus, the driver asked,"What the hell was all that about? Where are they?"

Marshall said, "Skip it. They won't be back."

The driver was beginning to feel a sense of injury. He said, "What's the matter with my bus all of a sudden? That's three guys. Had I better report in?"

Marshall laid a hand on his shoulder. "I wouldn't worry. Like, now there's nothing in the rules that says a guy's got to go on riding if he doesn't want to. Weirdos. Like I said, forget it."

The driver looked up into Marshall's face. *Smooth. Cool. Maybe he knew something that was nobody else's business. What the hell. So two guys got off and took taxis. Report what?* The driver said, "Okay, bud."

Marshall went back into the bus, passing Wilks, whose thoughts were somewhat different. *Dangerous! If that son of a bitch starts anything he'll be the first to get it between the eyes.*

As the bus moved off and Marshall was back in his seat, Julian asked, "What happened? W-w-where did they go?"

Marshall replied, "Nothing," and then realizing that the boy was too bright to be fobbed off, made the motion of closing his lips with a zipper and whispered, "Secret agents maybe."

Wide-eyed, Julian said, "Gee, honest? Spies?"

Marshall did the zipper movement again and thought to himself, looking at the diagram in Julian's lap, *Now what the hell did that scared little monkey want with a picture of this? Had the man with the camera goofed too?* But then Marshall remembered that the Colonel had always seemed to be working on things on his lap. The fellow had had plenty of time to make his pictures but apparently had waited for Julian's advent to make his move. Aloud he said, "You sure the Colonel said this would work?"

Julian nodded, "Uh huh. See there, he said I c-c-could move that b-b-back and I said to put another w-w-washer. It'll be okay that way. Look, he gave me his address in W-W-Washington."

Marshall glanced at the card. So, he had been right about the Colonel being in Ordnance. Then he returned to studying the diagram. "So, you pull the trigger and what happens?"

Julian said, "Like I told you, b-b-bubbles come out."

Marshall repeated, "Bubbles come out. Yeah, I got that the first time." *And for this that dopey little man had almost got himself shot in the ass with a .45.* For a moment his mind went wild. What were the bubbles? Nerve gas? Poison? The kid was being used like Rudyard Kipling's Kim. Kim was used by the British in THE GREAT GAME as a spy. He said to himself, *Oh, for sweet Jesus' sake, Marshall, be yourself. Like the Colonel said, there was some kind of foul-up which could cost him his eagles and none of it's your business. The point is he said this thing will work and gave the kid his card. The boy really has something.* Aloud he said, "I call that pretty damn smart. When I was a kid I was always tinkering myself. I was gonna be an engineer."

Julian asked, "Did you invent anything?"

Marshall shook his head in negation.

Julian asked, "What happened?"

Marshall touched the battle jacket on his lap and for a moment a look of anger flashed across his face as he picked it up and irritably stuffed it down on the seat beside him. He replied, "Nothing," and then his countenance regained its usual bland expression as he added, "But just you stay with it, kid. You'll get somewhere."

He glanced at the drawing again and leaned back in his seat, his head tilted, his eyes staring blankly in long faraway thought.

7

It was dusk, lights had begun to come on and they had just passed through the main street of a small community consisting of a post office, a cafeteria, a Western Union office, a few stores and a motel. The place was called Indian Falls and no stop was scheduled there. Nevertheless, the bus had come to a halt at the other side of town where there seemed to be some kind of a barrier across the road and a confusion of people gathered there. The bus was out of Arizona and into New Mexico and the wild country and at the foot of the pass that led over the Black Range to the valley of the Rio Grande.

Marshall said, "Now what?"

Julian, who had been indulging once

more in the sweet dream of his father confessing for the hundredth time that he had misjudged him and was proud of him, came out of it and asked, "Is something wrong?"

Marshall said, "I dunno. There seems to be some kind of a roadblock."

There was a sheriff's car at the barrier, some townspeople standing about. The bus driver got out and walked over as the noise of distant motorcycles was heard and everyone looked up in the direction of the road signposted INDIAN FALLS PASS as two state troopers came roaring down, got off their cycles and talked to the man in the sheriff's car, pantomiming with their hands as they told their story. The bus driver, now surrounded by bystanders, talked with the troopers briefly, consulted the Sheriff for a moment and then returned to his bus where he picked up his microphone connecting him by radio to the main Dispatcher's Office and, cupping the mouthpiece with his hand, spoke *sotto voce* for a minute or so. Thereafter he transferred to his interior mike and addressed his passengers.

"Folks, I'm sorry, but there's been a washout and landslide twelve miles up Indian Falls Pass and they say we can't get through. The troopers say there's a gang working on it and they expect to have it cleared by morning. So, here's the news, folks. We're staying overnight at the company's expense. There's a nice motel here, dinner's on the house, eat all you like. You'll be comfortable. Okay, everybody pile out."

Marshall said, "Well, whaddya know, a night in the sack. That suits me," and then he added, almost too hastily, "Can you look after yourself?"

If Julian was disappointed at Marshall's question he did not show it. A room all to himself in a motel was pretty exciting too. Maybe there'd even be a TV set in it and no one to tell him to turn it off and go to bed. He said, "Aw, sure. I got my case."

Marshall said, "Okay, kid, see you in the morning," and was one of the first off the bus. Overnight with Julian asking eternal questions had not been attractive and he had thought suddenly about Clyde Gresham and was thankful that he had scared him off the bus.

As people were reaching for overnight bags and pressing down the aisle, Bill looked at Marge. They were still in their seats. He was conscious of a sudden excitement. He was no longer called upon to make a decision. The situation had been taken out of their hands. This was where they were going to spend the night and, as far as he knew, nobody had ever heard of a place called Indian Falls. He put his arm about Marge's shoulder and whispered, "I guess here, maybe. Yeah?"

For Marge the decision had been made too and that it had happened without their having done anything more about it served somehow to quiet her qualms. There was no turning back now. She nodded in assent, leaned her head for a moment so that her hair touched Bill's cheek to reassure him. Then they retrieved their overnight gear and joined the end of the line of passengers. Julian, too, lagged behind, fascinated by the sheriff's black-and-white car and troopers with their big guns and shining cartridge belts and the single street of the small town that was almost like a movie set.

The sign read INDIAN FALLS MOTEL, R. GRADY. PROP., and the motel name was repeated in varicolored electric light bulbs that blinked on and off. It was a rather fair-sized establishment since, although Indian Falls was no great shakes of a metropolis, in fact hardly a dot on the map, tourists coming through at nightfall preferred to stay there and run the twisting roads of the pass in the morning. R. Grady was known as Pop and naturally his wife was Mom. Pop had been dried out by the sun until he was as stringy and tough as a slab of jerked deer meat. Mom, on the other hand, had two Mexican girls to do all the dirty work and so had blown up into a rotund and comfortable butterball with three chins and specs worn mostly on top of her head.

The cabins were gathered, in a U-curve, around the court in which there were planted flowers and cactus and yucca, with the office at one end of the U and the dining room at the other.

Behind the counter Pop booked the passengers in, and Mom billowing over a high stool handed out the keys. At the end of the line Marge and Bill and Julian were waiting to be assigned rooms, with Julian barely visible over the top of the counter. Neither Mom nor Pop noticed him.

Pop looked queryingly at Marge and Bill, spotted the ring on Marge's finger and said, "Mr. and Mrs. . . . ?" He looked up at them and when neither said anything, chortled, "Newlyweds," and then to Marge, "You're gonna have to get used to having your name changed, ma'am. Never mind, the room's on the bus company anyway. Mr. and Mrs. Newlywed." He turned to his wife. "Number twenty-five, Mom."

Mom said, "Welcome, folks. Now, where did that number twenty-five get to? I thought I had it in my hand." She began a search for the missing key which seemed to be neither in its box nor on the counter before her. ". . . I could of swore I had it in my hand."

Pop said, "Use your specs, Mom. You're blind as an old gopher without 'em." Quite suddenly he became aware of carroty hair, a forehead and half a pair of steel-rimmed glasses showing above the counter. Julian was standing on tiptoes so that he would be noticed.

Pop said, "Well, hello, buster. Where did you come from?"

Julian replied, "The bus. C-c-can I have a room, p-p-please?"

"Ain't you with nobody?"

Julian shook his head in negation.

Pop glanced at the key rack. "Right now it looks like we're fresh out of rooms. Ain't that so, Mom?"

Mom was now engaged in frisking her ample person. "That's right. Every one's took. Now where did I put that dratted key?"

Pop said, "What do we do about this shaver here? Kid's all by hisself, but he's on the bus."

Mom leaned over the counter for a look at Julian. "All by hisself, is he? Well, there just ain't any more rooms." Suddenly she looked sharply at Marge and Bill and an edge crept into her voice. "Say? You two are a young married couple. You're gonna have to get used to kids sometime. How about taking him in with you? Number twenty-five's got a foldaway bed in it."

She had flipped her glasses down from the top of her head and from behind them her eyes glared at them. The boy and the girl could only exchange one miserable glance before Mom challenged them again. "Well?"

Marge said, "Alright, you can put him in with us."

Mom said, "Well, that's right nice of you. Oh, for land's sakes, here's the key all the time right in my pocket. Now what on earth did I put it there for? Here you are." She handed it to Bill and then said to Julian, "There. Now you go along with them, sonny. You got any luggage?"

As Julian exhibited his little suitcase Bill had moved Marge off to one side and fiercely angry, muttered, "What the hell did you say yes for?"

Anguished, Marge replied, "Bill, what could I do? Don't you see? They saw this," and indicated the wedding ring. "If I'd said . . ."

Julian moved over to them. "Is it alright for me to come?" He looked so anxious and uncomfortable Marge went to him and put her arm about him. "Of course."

Pop said, "Number twenty-five's the nearest one. Right next to the office here. I'll show you how to work the bed."

In a photographic darkroom somewhere in a Southwestern city in the early evening three men were examining developed negatives and wet prints. They were smoking nervously and conversing in Russian.

The technician held up a print. He said, "Excellent. You have done well, Comrade Allon."

The courier, clad in black leather for a night motorcycle ride, his helmet dangling over one arm, inquired, "What is it? Is it important?"

Nikolas Allon replied, "Secret weapon. You know where to find the plane, Boris. It will be waiting. You will of course not fail."

The technician studied the picture again and asked, "What is this about soapy water and air bag?"

Allon replied, "Don't be stupid. Code. The KGB will break it in a few hours."

The technician carefully packed the finished work in plastic into a flat package and then wrapped it in waterproof linen. The courier stowed it away inside his leather jacket and sealed the pocket with tape. He asked, "Will there be pursuit?"

"Naturally," replied Allon.

The courier said, "What about this?" and indicated the small laboratory.

Allon remarked, "We won't be needing it again. It doesn't matter. When they find it, it will be too late."

All three went out of the darkroom. The technician locked the door and put the key in his pocket and they hurried down three flights of stairs to emerge from a shabby-looking loft building in the industrial part of town. There were pedestrians and mild traffic in the street but no one paid any attention to the three.

The courier straddled the latest model giant Honda and kicked it into life. They shook hands and Allon said, "Good luck, Comrade."

The technician and Allon turned away and merged with the passersby. The courier gunned his machine and shot off. When he reached the outskirts of the city he turned off his lights and became one with the darkness.

With the foldaway cot let down beside the big double bed, and with a giant color television set, the bureau and an overstuffed chair, there was hardly space to move in

Room 25 or get to the bathroom. As a matter of fact there was no path at all leading to the foldaway except directly across the double bed, which it joined so closely that the mattresses touched.

Supper had been a success. Mom and Pop had been generous with their food and there were Mexican tidbits. Afterwards Julian, on his best behavior, had prepared himself for the night, brushing his teeth vigorously and loudly and then appearing in his pajamas. Bill slouched unhappily in the overstuffed chair, Marge sat on the arm.

Julian gazed longingly at the big color set. He said, "C-c-can we look at TV?"

Marge began doubtfully, "Well . . ." She felt that she had let Bill down, had been perhaps too quick to take the kid in with them. What could the proprietor have done if they had refused?

Bill cut in curtly, "No, we can't," and then rather more placatingly, "Look here, Julian, it's been a long day. We're all tired. You better get into bed."

Julian hadn't expected that he would be allowed to watch the box. That had gone down the drain along with the dream of the room to himself. And so he said amiably, "Okay."

He studied the layout for a moment. There was no route to reach the foldaway except cross-country. He leaped up onto the big double bed which turned out to be well sprung and enticingly bouncy. In effect, and in Julian's mind, a kind of trampoline. He took three bounces, each one higher than the last, to land with a chortle of delight on his bed where he cried, "Say, that's great," and settled himself between the sheets.

Marge could not bear to look at Bill. Something way deep down inside of her wanted to laugh.

Bill said, "Go to sleep. We'll put the light out."

Julian answered, "Alright. Thanks for everything. You're swell. Good night."

Marge felt as though she ought to go to him and give him a good-night comfort of some kind, a pat, a kiss, a cuddle, but she was halted by two visions of herself, one bouncing across the bed to get to him, the other making the crossing on her hands and knees. The deeply buried laugh pushed a little harder. Marge pushed back and said to Julian, "Good night. Sleep tight."

Julian smiled, removed his glasses which made him look suddenly extraordinarily touching, young and vulnerable, put his head to the pillow and was off.

Bill got up and flipped the light and the room was now illuminated only by the reflection of the electric advertising sign of the motel. The two sat on the edge of the double bed, but with some distance between them and when they spoke it was in whispers.

Marge asked, "Bill, are you angry with me? I'm sorry."

"No, I guess not."

Marge looked over at the sleeping boy and murmured, "He's sweet."

Bill said, "He's a pest."

Marge said, "Bill, do you think . . . I mean, should we . . . ?"

"Ssshhhh! Wait 'til we're sure the kid's asleep."

They sat waiting. Julian had indeed dropped off immediately but now he stirred for the first time lightly and then was quiet. Bill looked across inquiringly at Marge and reached for her hand. She withdrew it, shaking her head in negation, but softened the rejection by putting her finger to her lips.

Bill momentarily felt drained of all excitement. He was no longer angry with Marge but with his life pattern. He was not a lucky boy. Things had a way of getting screwed up with him whenever he embarked on any kind of project. He was bowed down by the ever pursuing fates. *Jesus, why did I have to get into a thing like this? It wouldn't happen to anybody else.*

The two sat waiting and watching the sleeping child.

The two cars roared up to the loft building and disgorged Army Intelligence and three FBI men. Colonel Sisson, still hugging his unstolen briefcase, was with them. He said, "This the place?" and an FBI man said, "Uh huh." They stormed up the stairs and down a corridor to a numbered room. The glass pane on the door read "Cosmo Co., Inc." The FBI man said, "This is it," and tried the door.

Sisson ordered viciously, "Kick it in." They did and pushed in, flipping on a light. All his life the Colonel had been prey to the most curious fantasies in moments of stress like wanting to cry like a child when Allon had escaped him. Now the words that flashed through his mind were, "The birds have flown."

They had indeed. The men burst into the deserted darkroom where they found all the evidence of developing and printing, and so recent that the odor of the chemicals had not yet evaporated.

Sisson asked, "You sure this is the place?"

The leader of the FBI men said, "We've had this place under surveillance."

Sisson remarked bitterly, "Some surveillance."

The FBI man said, "How the hell did we know it was going to happen the way you told it?"

They went downstairs again and when they came out a third car was just drawing up. A young Lieutenant of Army G2 hailed them and said, "We think they've got a small plane in a field on the outskirts. Someone saw it, but nobody seems to know about it. Brubaker's farm."

Sisson inquired, "Do you know where that is?"

The Lieutenant said, "Sort of."

"Well, come on then, what the hell are we waiting for?"

They piled back into their cars, the Lieutenant leading, and drove off. In the FBI vehicle, the agents looked to their automatic weapons.

The blinking motel sign had been extinguished, the room was now in darkness except for a glimmer from a street lamp whose light, via the open window, also fell athwart the sleeping Julian. Marge and Bill had managed somehow to get themselves into their nightclothes and were standing facing one another tremulously uncertain, nervous, Marge in a pretty gown, Bill all buttoned up in pajama top and bottom.

Bill said, "Gee, Marge, you look beautiful."

"Oh, Bill, do I?"

"He's asleep now."

Bill wasn't aware that he had opened his arms, nor Marge that she had moved into them and close to him, and thus for a moment they clung to one another and each experienced something they never had before, not so much those recognizable symptoms of young appetite and desire, but rather a most curious surge of tenderness, moving and different, as though each had found within the other and in themselves as well, an emotion they had not known or ever suspected was there.

Then they parted from one another for a moment shyly and with curiosity and wonder. Bill got into bed and moved over, so that he was near to the sleeping Julian. Hesitantly, and with a glance over towards the child, Marge joined him. The air-conditioning made it cool enough and they pulled up the covers but not touching lay there side by side, stiff and petrified as a pair of mummies, afraid to move. And somehow the magic of the discovery they had made that instant before was gone.

Bill was nervous and worried again. How was it then that one opened this game? He whispered, "I love you, Marge."

The girl too was prey to her moment of terror and doubt and all the fears that crowd up in the young and inexperienced, but she replied dutifully, "I love you too." And each still remained rigid.

Something had to give. Bill put out a tentative arm. He was reaching for Marge's shoulder but touched her breast.

With a quick intake of breath, the girl whispered, "Bill, please, no."

"Why?"

"What if he wakes up?"

"He won't wake up."

The feel of the soft flesh beneath the nylon gown made him bolder and Bill turned to reach for her. Julian suddenly moved violently in his sleep, his left arm was flung out and hit Bill a resounding thwack across the ear.

Bill, startled, yelled, "Hey, what the hell . . . ?" And Marge, in panic, shifted all the way over to the far edge of the bed.

Bill sat up, rubbed his ear, removed Julian's arm and turned him over so that his back was to them.

Closer inspection showed that the assault had been no more than a reflex action of Julian turning in his sleep and the boy continued dead out.

Bill muttered, "Oh, for godssake," and then moved across the big bed towards Marge, "It's okay. He isn't awake. Please, Marge."

"Are you sure?"

Bill said, "You couldn't wake him with a cannon."

Marge made a tentative move to abandon the sanctuary of the far side but not a great one. After that first moment of fright she had a clear memory of wondering exactly what she was doing there in a strange bed in a strange room with, in effect, a strange boy whom she did not really know all that well and, above all, why?

Bill's heart was filled with the fury of frustration. He had managed to get over the hurdle of that first tremendous move and it had not been a conspicuous success. He did not know how to gather himself to do it again. He was spared.

Julian stirred, woke up and said, "Mom?" and sat up in bed and looked about him confused for a moment as to where he was. The boy and girl put distance between them again.

Julian said, "Oh, I thought I was home for a minute."

Marge put her feet to the floor and sat up. "Yes, Julian, what is it?"

"I've g-g-got to go to the bathroom."

Bill said, "Oh, for Pete's sake, why didn't you go before? Hurry up, then."

Julian got up, took two preliminary bounces on his own cot and then did his trampoline act across the double bed and disappeared.

Bill thought to himself, *Oh my God, what if we were on our honeymoon?* But then he thought, too, that he wasn't on any honeymoon but only upon an exploratory voyage into the so-called mysteries of sex which suddenly was making him both look foolish and feel foolish. Trying to seem masculine, compelling and excited did not appear to go hand in hand. What a mess!

Julian emerged from the bathroom and varied his act with a run, one bounce and a three-point landing on his own bed. He said, "Thanks," and was asleep immediately.

Bill made another half-hearted attempt, whispering, "It's alright now. C'mon back to bed, Marge."

The girl took her feet from the floor but kept them curled up under her as, still sitting up, she found the courage to say, "Oh, Bill, can't you see this isn't the way we wanted it. Please . . . please . . ."

He was not angry any more but filled only with a sudden sense of relief. He had not failed, but then he had not been called upon to prove anything either and it was she who had let him off the hook. He sat up in the dark and looked across at the unhappy girl. A ray from the street touched her brow and showed the shadow of her tumbled hair. She looked different by lamplight and strange. He said with a kind of half-grudging grace, "Okay."

Marge said, "I'm sorry. I'm sort of all mixed up and tired."

"That's alright, Marge. Go to sleep."

"You're not angry?"

"No. Honest."

Marge leaned over to kiss him gently on his temple but in the darkness missed and caught the side of his nose. Her hair tumbled about his face. He kissed back and got an eye.

He said, "Good night, Marge. Sleep well."

Marge whispered back, "Good night," and then barely audibly, "And thank you, Bill."

All her fears and doubts allayed, the innocence of sleep was upon Marge within a few moments. She had been let off from something she knew now that she had not really wanted, at least not on these terms, egged on by the actions and opinions of outsiders who had nothing to do with her, or who or what she was. Another day, another year; that self that, by the grace of one small boy, she had been given a few critical moments to reevaluate had been preserved in her.

Bill lay awake a moment longer and thought, *Oh boy, if the gang ever finds out I went to bed with a girl and didn't do anything,* and then quite suddenly he felt so young, younger even than the child sleeping soundly next to him, and he was filled with the sense of something found and then lost and knew that it would be perhaps a long time before he would find it again. He was too old to shed the tears that were there because of the misery that had caught at his throat. Instead, he murmured bravely, "Oh, hell," rolled over and joined the other two in oblivion.

Under half moonlight partially obscured by scudding clouds, and outlined slightly by the glow from a distant city, a light plane sat at one end of a long, fenced-in, neglected field of rough grass and weeds, a dangerous runway, bordered by clumps of trees. A spark of light came from the pilot's cigarette cupped in his hand as he waited. In flying suit and leather helmet he sat on a wing, smoked and listened. When he heard the first distant throbbing of a motorcycle he glanced at his wristwatch, stubbed out the butt, leaned into the cockpit, switched on and swung his propeller so that the machine shuddered into life and strained against the chocks under the wheels. Right on time.

There was no doubt, he thought, that the bastards, whoever they were, were efficient as well as good-paying. The fact that he was letting his country down did not worry him one bit. The country, in his opinion, was letting itself down faster than he ever could, besides which all that cloak-and-dagger crap was a lot of kid stuff and little ever seemed to come of it. At any rate, they were on schedule. The racket of the approaching motorcycle grew louder, then it came leaping and bumping across the field to the plane, the rider pulling a packet from his pocket even before he had dismounted.

The pilot stowed the package, climbed into the cockpit, leaned out and said, "Pull those stones out from
under my wheels and then get out of the way fast and you
better get your ass out of here quick. I see lights of cars
coming."

The chocks removed, the pilot held his plane for a
moment with his brake to give the courier time to duck
out of the way, leap onto his cycle and drive off.

Even over the steady hum of his propeller, for he had
warmed up earlier, the pilot could now hear the rolling
grind of fast motorcars approaching and saw the glare of
their headlights around a bend. He gave his ship full
throttle.

The field was uneven and bumpy and he needed every
bit of power, but he saw clearly enough to avoid rocks
and furrows as the clouds parted for a moment. The little
ship bounced and swayed. A stone fence at the end of the
field rushed at him but by then he was able to risk yank-
ing her up off the ground. He flew level for a moment or
two to pick up power just as three cars roared up to the
side of the field and disgorged angry men. The pilot
stayed even with the trees at one side of the field, using
them for cover to gain still more flying speed. Then he
pulled her up, banked sharply and as the clouds again cut
down illumination, vanished into the night sky.

On the ground, Colonel Sisson watched in helpless
frustration and one of the FBI men released a burst of
absolutely useless machine-gun fire into the nowhere
which echoed mockingly from a derelict farm a short
distance away until Sisson said in disgust, "Oh, for
chrissakes, cut it out, he's gone."

The young Lieutenant, who saw himself wearing a single bar for the rest of his life, said, "My God, Colonel, I'm sorry I took you to the wrong field first but there wasn't anything too definite."

Sisson felt sorry for him. This was obviously going to be the pattern, lousy intelligence, bad luck, rotten timing, always too late. He said, "Never mind. Not your fault. We've got to get in touch with the Air Force."

In the morning Marge was already out of bed and dressed when Bill awoke and sheepishly climbed into his clothing. Julian was in the bathroom from which the sound of running shower and tremendous splashing was heard. Bill, searching for his shoes, was distracted by the sounds, fell over Julian's suitcase and kicked it hard with his bare foot. The suitcase took no injury except to be lofted a few feet but Bill was now hopping around hanging onto his big toe and yelling in pain, "Goddamn little bastard!"

He caught sight of Marge, who appeared to be in the grip of something extraordinary; she looked as though she might be going to be sick or something. But it was only the deep-down laugh that had begun the night before which now could no longer be controlled. Furiously Bill became aware that Marge was beginning to break up and at her first peal of almost hysterical laughter his own rage evaporated and he began to giggle himself and in a moment they fell into one another's arms laughing until they were weak.

When at last they had exhausted themselves and parted, Marge regarded Bill with an expression of wry maturity. She said, "Bill, do you mind? I want to go home."

Bill, too, had grown up. He said, "Yeah, I guess you're right. We could get a bus back. Do you think they'll give us breakfast too?"

The bathroom door opened with dramatic suddenness and Julian made a magnificent appearance framed in it, all fresh and bright and washed. He shouted, "Hi, I'm ready!"

There was breakfast and when the passengers had finished and emerged from the motel they saw the Sheriff's men removing the ROAD CLOSED signs and the barriers, and a state trooper on a motorcycle appeared from the direction of the pass followed by an Inter-State bus displaying its destination sign, SAN DIEGO. It pulled up alongside Bus 396, the two drivers exchanged a few words about the condition of the road and the passengers streamed back on board. Marge, Bill and Julian were the last to appear, Julian still munching on half a muffin. The driver said, "Okay, kids, come on, shake it up," but only Julian climbed up on the step to the door and turned to look back.

Marge came over, reached up and gave him a kiss. She said, "Goodbye, Julian, and thank you."

Julian, looking down upon her, was slightly baffled and embarrassed and asked, "What for?"

Bill held out his hand and said, "Good luck with the invention. Be seeing you sometime." He and Marge turned towards the San Diego-bound bus.

The driver called after them, "Hey, what's with you two? Aren't you going on?"

Bill turned and called back, "We changed our minds."

The driver used the fingers of his right hand for counting, "That makes one-two-three-four-five. What's the matter with my bus? Of all the loony trips."

Marshall let Julian have the window seat as the bus moved off. He said, "How was it? Sleep okay last night?"

Julian replied, "G-g-great. There weren't any more rooms and I had to g-g-go with Marge and Bill."

Marshall gave Julian a long and quizzical look. He said, "You did? What happened?"

Julian replied, "Nothing. They were nice. There was an extra bed in a closet that came out." He suddenly grinned in recollection. "I had to b-b-bounce over them."

Marshall said, "They must have enjoyed that."

"Aw, they didn't care."

Marshall, still studying Julian half amused, was visualizing the scene and wondering exactly what had happened and whether Julian had had any suspicion as he himself had that this was not a honeymoon pair at all but a couple of kids getting away from home for a lay. He thought probably not. It was this quality of innocence in Julian which somehow had touched him. Wise-guy, smart-aleck children he couldn't bear. In this day and age most of them were. He said, "What made them suddenly decide to turn around and go back to San Diego?"

"I dunno. They didn't say."

"And you didn't ask?"

Julian looked at him in astonishment. "What for?"

Marshall laughed. "Kid, if you go on minding your own business like that you'll go far."

8

The pilot of the light plane had just
spotted the distant fringe of coast in the
early morning light with its white band
of gently breaking Pacific surf barely
visible when the two searching Army
jets picked up his blips on their radar
and soon had him in eye range, a tiny
moth flying at five thousand feet.

The first jet pilot tuned his radio to
the private commercial band and spoke
into his microphone, "Piper Number
VN 473, do you read me?"

He repeated, "Piper Number VN 473,
do you read me?" He received no reply
but thought he saw a change in the
direction and angle of flight of the light
plane. He spoke again into his mike and
said, "Okay, mister, it's your hard luck

if you don't read me. Go down and land before we shoot you down. Those are orders."

The man in the cockpit of the Piper's cabin grimaced. There was the packet to deliver, the big pay handout, but it was also a silly way to die. He took a quick note of his position, the coastline and a stretch of flat beach vacated by the tide. He also saw something which he was convinced the pursuing jets might very well see but would not think about. Their job was simply to get him out of the air. He picked up his microphone and tuned to the military frequency. He said, "I read you. Okay. Roger. Wilco. I'm going down. Don't get nervous, boys."

He kicked the right rudder and put his plane into a side slip and dropped like an express elevator while the two jets descended to the level he had vacated. With the ground looming he kicked the rudder again, yanked the stick back and fishtailed onto the strip of beach. The hovercraft that had been waiting in the shallows sent up a spume of spray as it darted in-shore and nosed onto the beach.

The man in the Piper climbed out of his cockpit, threw one glance overhead to make sure that the jets hadn't followed him down into shooting range, ran to the hovercraft and handed his packet to the man waiting at the open door. He received an envelope in exchange. The door slammed, the hovercraft backed off and then stirred the Pacific into a real froth as with all engines full out and propellers whirring it roared off southbound. The hovercraft caught the jets totally by surprise and it was several minutes before they realized what had happened. The second pilot in a blaze of anger put his ship into a dive, yelling, "Why the son of a bitch!" into his microphone. He prepared his rockets for firing and at a thousand feet got the hovercraft into his crosshairs.

The first pilot chased him down and shouted into his mike, "Cool it, Johnny, for chrissakes. We're over Mexico. You gonna declare war all by yourself?"

The scene in the office of Lieutenant King was the same as it had been before except that with the Lieutenant absent Sergeant Cassidy, looking slightly grieved, was taking the brunt of West's angry voice heard emerging from the receiver held some distance from his ear.

When the shouting had somewhat subsided the Sergeant said, "I'm sorry, sir, I'm afraid not yet . . . Yeah, yeah, I know there was a bit of a mix-up on the description but we've got it right now and it's being broadcast every hour. I'm sorry about Mrs. West being took sick in bed but we oughta have some news any minute. See, you never know with these kids when they're on the lam . . . No, no, sir, I didn't mean that. Sure he ain't on the lam. But we figure on them hitchhiking and sooner or later the driver tunes in for the news and we've got him . . . Sure, sure, we're checking on all the airports and terminals. The kid wouldn't be going to Honolulu on a hundred and fifty bucks, would he? . . . No, no, Mr. West, I ain't tryin' to be fresh. It's only we got everybody workin' on this. We'll call you as soon as we hear anything."

It was the sheer coziness of the atmosphere aboard Bus 396 which at least temporarily spared Julian from the searching efforts of Sergeant Cassidy for the Sergeant had done his duty and notified all rail and bus terminals as well as police, state-trooper and sheriff offices in the vicinity. Luck and the bus driver's preoccupation with the curious melting away of his passengers also helped Julian evade capture, for when the dispatcher in Oklahoma City had routinely warned him to keep his eye out for a child traveling alone, the driver was still mulling over the mystery of his defecting passengers, and a further fact was that, except for a glimpse during the boarding at San Diego, he had never seen Julian actually traveling alone. The driver was not an intellectual giant and tooling one of those monsters across the continent called for the most intense concentration. The fact that one of the kids on his bus had been with three different parties failed to register. He had always appeared under the care of somebody.

And none of the passengers seemed interested in the news broadcasts.

It was shortly after two o'clock, the bus rolling at seventy miles an hour, a half hour beyond Lordsburg bound for El Paso, that Julian's incognito was to be violently destroyed.

There had been a short halt at Lordsburg for the passengers to buy luncheon and Marshall had treated handsomely. They had changed seats again with Marshall by the window. Julian had a hamburger roll in one hand, a bottle of Coke in the other and on his lap a paper plate containing a sticky cream puff and a Mars bar.

Marshall was munching a ham and cheese on rye and washing it down with a can of beer. His paper plate had apple pie and a slab of cheese on it. Elsewhere all over the bus luncheon parties were going on with the exception of the chess players who, now with only a few pieces remaining, were pursuing one another over the squares with increasing ferocity.

Julian finished his hamburger and got his nose into the cream puff. He said, "Say, this is great. Thanks a lot. I was all out of tuna fish. Can I pay you for what you spent?"

Marshall said, "No, that's alright, this one's on me," and as Julian got deeper into his cream puff and acquired a fetching white moustache, Marshall regarded him once more with a mixture of curiosity and, in spite of his desire for noninvolvement, with a strange growing affection. He said, "Look here, Julian, this crazy caper of yours. What about when you get to Washington? How much money have you got?"

"Fifty dollars. My grandmother gave me a hundred and fifty for my b-b-birthday."

Marshall snorted, "Fifty bucks! You know how far that will go?"

Julian shook his head and Marshall continued, "Look, I've got my last five hundred on me but in a town like Washington it might just as well be your fifty. If I don't connect with a job when I get there I'll be flat." He grinned suddenly at Julian and said, "I guess you and me are in the same boat. Me and my kid brother. Both on our asses. Isn't that something?" And then as Julian regarded him worshipfully, he became serious and said, "Kidding aside, what do you do when the fifty is gone?"

Julian thought that this was a stupid question and the tone of voice in which he replied indicated that. He said, "Sell my Bubble Gun. The Colonel said it would work. I'll have my p-p-patent . . ."

In a sudden burst of exasperation Marshall cried,

"Work, work, work! For chrissakes, kid, wake up. Don't you see you can't just go barging . . ."

Here Marshall cut off without finishing his speech of admonition about the futility of Julian's quest, for suddenly looking up towards the front of the bus his eyes had caught a glimpse of something that was not as it should be and that subliminal sense of danger not yet eroded by more than a year of civilian life again was there to warn him. He said, "Now, what the hell is going on up there?"

Sam Wilks was a psychopathic killer, a piece of white trash turned thief and murderer. By almost incredible luck he had avoided the police dragnet at San Diego where he had been expected to try to get across the border at Tijuana. After robbing and killing a gas station attendant at Carlsbad between Los Angeles and San Diego, he had abandoned his stolen getaway car and vanished. There had apparently been no witnesses to the crime and there had been no accurate description of him available but everything pointed to his crossing over into Mexico. Nobody had either expected or looked for him on an eastbound bus.

Hunched in the front seat of the upper level of Bus 396, his hat pulled down over his eyes, a map of the district in front of him, Wilks was full of himself and the Godlike feeling of knowing he was master of life and death. He had got away with it and he would still vanish into the badlands of Mexico until the heat was off. He carried two articles on his person which practically guaranteed this. One was a .45 automatic pistol, the other a hand grenade of a new Army mark, a recently introduced model with the explosive force of a three-inch shell. The stability of this latter horror, from which Wilks always kept the pin half pulled, was no more reliable than the man holding it. He belonged to that new breed of self-justified terrorists spawned in the seventies and like all of them was prepared to risk everything including himself, with the cunning to let the dice roll on the gamble of trying something never before attempted.

His map showed him that they were approaching the small town of Deming, about an hour or so from El Paso and Ciudad Juarez, Mexico. The authorities would not be looking for him coming from that direction and even if they were no one was going to stop him. He folded up the map, having committed to memory the spot where a secondary road branched off, put it away in his pocket, pushed back his hat to mop his brow for only the briefest moment of nerves, which he shed by thinking that he would probably kill that good-looking son of a bitch who had been interfering with him and enjoy doing it. His right hand closed around the warm steel butt of the .45. His left hand curled against the fragmentation squares of the grenade in his pocket. He turned around once for a last look at the disposition of the passengers, where they were and what they were doing, another glimpse of the bus driver and the road ahead, and then made his move.

Julian said, "What? Going on up where?"

Marshall said, "I dunno. Sit still." But he thought he did know, for having half risen out of his seat so that he could look over the heads of the other passengers he saw the character in the dirty clothes and ten-gallon hat get up, go forward and lean over the shoulder of the bus driver. He was holding something in his right hand, a second object in his left, and Marshall had no difficulty recognizing either of them.

Between his teeth Marshall muttered, "The son of a bitch," and without a weapon felt completely naked and helpless and at the same time very angry. He watched the bus driver momentarily take his eyes from the road and stare up at the man Wilks with utter incredulity and then with a shaking hand pick up the microphone connecting him with headquarters.

The main Dispatcher's Office of the company in Oklahoma City was a vast air-conditioned, soundproof chamber filled with receiving and sending apparatus and men and girls serving it as the messages came pouring in from every corner of the country. At the end of the room there was a huge map of the United States with all the bus routes, and the messages were relayed to boys there who stuck pins and flags into the routes so that an overseer at a glimpse would know practically where every one of his vehicles might be within fifty miles at any given time. At the other end of the room the Chief Dispatcher sat at a high desk like a judge's bench with earphones and a plug-in switchboard which could connect him with any of the incoming or outgoing circuits. The room was filled with the quiet hum of the voices of the dispatchers speaking *sotto voce,* livened by occasional interference crackle where somebody was encountering weather.

At one of the receiving desks the instrument gave a

long bleep and then came the muffled mechanical tone of a voice adulterated by electronics, "Three nine six, three nine six. Do you read me? Three nine six."

The dispatcher put on his headset with a yawn, but then suddenly looking up at the big electric clock on the wall, wondered what the hell 396 was calling him for at that hour. He adjusted a dial for better reception and said, "Three nine six. I read you, Mike. What's cooking?" and then his eyes popped as a voice clearly said, "We're ten miles west of Deming. I've got a guy with a gun on me."

"You got what?"

The bus driver's voice said, "He's going to take us down from Deming to the border. He wants to cross at Juarez Oeste. And half a million bucks. He says he wants half a million bucks. He's got a bomb. He says he'll blow us all up."

To the dispatcher it could be nothing more than a gag or maybe Mike had got loaded somewhere, but if he was that kind of a goddamned fool the Chief Dispatcher ought to know about it. He pressed a button at his desk and a red light glowed on the panel by the Chief Dispatcher's rostrum. The Chief threw a switch and donned earphones and microphone.

The dispatcher spoke a curt message to his superior, "Three nine six claims he's been hijacked," and then to the bus said, "Aw, listen, you're kiddin', ain't you? You trying to say you got a hijacker on board? C'mon Mike, what is this? Cut out the clowning. Nobody hijacks a bus."

Even though distorted by electronics the fear and tension could be heard raising the pitch of the driver's voice. "Oh, my God, listen, will you. He's letting me get through to tell you to keep the cops off and he ain't kidding. I got a .45 in my ear and a bomb at the back of my neck. And, listen, he says the half a million in small bills. It's to be waiting at the U.S. Immigration Station at West El Paso."

The Chief spoke into his microphone and said, "This is Olson, Chief Dispatcher. Look here . . ."

The driver's voice rose to a near hysterical pitch. "I don't care who it is. He's saying a cop comes within twenty yards of the bus and the thing he's got goes bang. He says it's one of them new grenades that'll kill everybody on board. I got twenty-one adults and three kids."

The Chief said, "Okay, okay, we believe you. Keep your cool. We'll do all we can to help you. Do the passengers know yet?"

Three nine six said, "They will now," and clicked off.

Standing on the top step at the head of the second level of the bus, the .45 in one hand, the grenade in the other, facing half to the rear but angled so that he could threaten the driver as well as the passengers below him, Wilks was in complete control. He could watch the sides and the rear should pursuit develop and too, he had a glimpse of the driver's mirrors. He said to the driver, "Okay, bud, speak your piece."

One by one, in unbelieving horror, the passengers were becoming aware of the man with the gun and the grenade. The driver picked up his interior microphone. "Okay, folks, everybody please keep calm. Our friend here says he'd like to jump the border at Juarez and if you'll just kindly keep your seats he says how nobody ought to get hurt. We should be there in about an hour. Is that right, Jack?"

Wilks laughed and said, "Like you learned your little piece in school." And then, "You told them other fellows about the money, didn't you?"

The driver said, "You heard me."

Speaking loudly so as to be heard over the bus noises and the roar of the big wheels on the tarmac, Wilks said, "That's about the straight of it, folks. I don't aim to hurt nobody if you all stay where you are in your seats, but I wouldn't like this here thing to go off 'cause they sure make a powerful mess. And don't nobody try to get brave neither. See this here little pin?" He held up the grenade so that they could all see the clip pin at the side partly withdrawn from the ring holding it. "If this comes out the rest of the way, we all go." He laughed. "That's okay with me too, so don't get any ideas that I ain't got the guts to do it."

The bus erupted into fragmented sentences, little cries of alarm, notes of sheer incredulity.

"What's that? What'd he say?"

"Oh my God, he's got a gun and a bomb."

"What is it? A hijack?"

Wilks laughed, "You might call it that. First one on a bus. So, let's just keep nice and quiet on account of these here things are kind of nervous like," and he flipped the grenade in his hand.

A male passenger yelled, "Man, are you crazy? Whoever heard of hijacking a bus?"

And another, "It don't make no sense, feller. Why didn't you hijack an airplane?"

Wilks laughed again. "They don't buzz you for hardware at bus stations yet. Maybe I'm scared of airyplanes."

A woman came out with, "For land's sakes, ain't a body safe nowhere no more? I had half a mind to fly, only my daughter says to me, 'Don't you do it, Mom, with all them hijackers. You just go along on the bus and you'll get there safe and sound.' "

Wilks' sarcastic, irritating voice suddenly turned oily with exaggerated politeness. "Now, don't you worry for one minute, ma'am, and I'm mighty sorry to be disturbin' of you. After we part company, maybe in an hour or so, you'll git where yer goin' to sure enough."

One of the male passengers had half risen from his seat. "But, listen to reason, man, you can't get away with—"

Wilks leveled the .45. "Sit down and shut up." And his admonishment was unexpectedly followed up by one from Marshall not far away who cried sharply to the passenger, "Sir, sit down!"

The man turned and looked at him saying, "Say, are you one of the gang?"

Marshall said, "No, I'm not, but you don't argue with a hand grenade when there's a bus full of lives. Can't you see he's got the pin half out?"

Wilks looked over the heads of the passengers to catch Marshall's eye and called out sarcastically, "Well, now, Mister, ain't you smart. I'll bet yer one of them *he*-roes. Tell the folks what happens when one of these things goes off."

Marshall arose and said placatingly, "Listen, fella, you got a gun on us. Nobody's gonna start anything. What about getting rid of that grenade. There are women and children on this . . ."

Marshall's voice trailed off for a bitter, sour expression had come to Wilks' mouth and the big .45 was now leveled directly at Marshall's head.

The hijacker said, "Shut up and sit down. Don't try no *he*-ro stuff with me. You been in my hair already a coupla times and I'm figurin' on putting a bullet through your skull before I get off this bus. Maybe I'll do it right now."

Marshall went white and large beads of sweat appeared upon his brow. He remained standing, but Julian, looking at him with surprise, saw that he was holding to the sides of the seat in front of him.

Wilks laughed loudly, "Yer scared, ain't you?"

Marshall did not reply and Julian regarded him with sudden misery and a sense of overwhelming disappointment. There was no question about it. Marshall was indeed badly frightened but then Julian had no way of knowing that his friend was within a few seconds of being killed. Marshall had divined the hijacker as a psychopath, as dangerous and unstable as his bomb when the pin would be wholly removed.

As Wilks' trigger finger began to tighten the bus flashed by a small crossroads from which two state troopers on motorcycles roared out and turned onto the main highway in pursuit, momentarily distracting Wilks who, relinquishing the bead he had drawn on the center of Marshall's forehead, now concentrated on the discharge mechanism of the grenade and ordered the driver, "Tell them cops if they come any closer this thing goes off."

Somehow the antennae of a four-year-old girl picked up the sense of horror and danger permeating the interior of the bus and she began to cry, "Mommy,

Mommy." Her mother hugged the child to her and called out aloud, "Oh, you beast!"

At once Wilks became transformed again and he replied with exaggerated courtesy, "Why no, ma'am, don't talk like that. I ain't no beast. Why, I got kiddies of my own at home I wouldn't want to see no harm come to any more'n you would yours. I like kiddies and kiddies like me. That's a fact. You got nuthin' to be afraid of as long as nobody don't try nuthin' funny."

If the two chess players were aware of what was going on about them they gave no sign. The first offered one of his remaining pawns with an evil grin, the other with an equally wicked grin took it with a bishop which he immediately lost to a lurking knight he had overlooked. The bus had gone silent inside and at the rear one passenger whispered to another, "Keep quiet. I know the type. He's psychopathic. They're the worst. Oh, God, don't let him do it."

Marshall was still pale and tight-lipped and staring straight in front of him and, during the momentary distraction of the two police, had sat down. The appearance of the law he knew could make matters worse. One could smell the fear in him. Julian threw him another anguished look. That wasn't the way they behaved on TV.

Back in the Dispatcher's Office, the bus driver's circuit had been switched onto a loudspeaker. The Chief Dispatcher was connected with the police by telephone.

The bus driver's voice now came booming from the speaker and said, "Listen, will you. There are cops following us. Tell 'em to lay off. And no roadblocks. He says if there's a roadblock, he'll . . ."

The Chief Dispatcher repeated rapidly into his telephone, ". . . and he says not to try any roadblocks. Just tell your men to keep away from them."

The driver's voice boomed again, "He was gonna kill a passenger a minute ago because he didn't like his face."

"The driver says he's a killer," the Chief relayed into the mouthpiece. "We've got women and kids on that bus."

Again the bus driver: "He's asking what about the money."

The dispatcher quickly picked up the mike and said, "Tell him we're rounding it up."

Number 396 was approaching the crossroads. The west–east highway showed a sign: DEMING 1 MILE, EL PASO 60 MILES. The road leading off to the right was marked: HEAVY TRUCKS. MORELLOS 30 MILES. EL PASO 63 MILES. JUAREZ OESTE 65 MILES.

As the driver slowed for cross traffic, two more motorcycle policemen, a sheriff's car and two state troopers' vehicles could be seen at the side of the road, but they made no move. Wilks tapped the driver on the shoulder with his gun barrel and with his hand waved him to the right. Reluctantly the driver tugged at his heavy wheel and, picking up speed, he headed south. The troopers and police joined the cortege.

The bus driver had a try. He said, "Man, use your nut. You're crazy. When we get to Juarez them Mexican cops'll grab you."

Wilks laughed and flipped the grenade again, pretending to miss it before catching it. "Haw! Not with this they won't. You talk into that thing and tell 'em to fix it up

with them greasers on the other side to lay off me, see?
And the dough gets handed to me this side of the border."

At police headquarters in Oklahoma City, a police captain was snapping orders into the telephone. "I want the
road cleared through to the border. Get it? There'll be
a man there with the money . . . No, no, no! For chris-
sake, don't try anything, you fools. And tell that goddamned FBI if there's a shoot-out they'll have the blood
of these passengers and kids on their hands."

He listened for a moment and then repeated with em-
phasis, "You heard me. I said no! This man is a dangerous lunatic. We've contacted the Mexicans at Juarez
Oeste, but you better cover the main border station and
El Paso as well. We'll worry about the international end
of it later. I want outriders at the front, say at fifty yards
to clear the way, and no one to approach closer than that.
I'm holding you responsible."

By this time 396 had picked up an escort of some thirty
motorcycles and state troopers' cars following at the required distance. Ahead another squadron of troopers
were clearing the way, waving trucks and cars to the side
of the road. Above a helicopter clattered.

The size of the escort and the utter helplessness in the
face of his power was obviously giving Wilks pleasure
and he could not keep a half smirk of self-satisfaction
from his face. The bus entered, and was about to roll
down the long main street of the fairly sizable town of
Morellos. The way had been cleared. Nothing moved in
the streets, local constables and sheriffs kept townspeo-

ple back and under control. The cortege roared through even more loudly as the sides of the brick and wooden buildings threw back an echo.

The smirk of self-admiration turned into one of amusement as they emerged from the other side of town. Wilks said, "Well now, wasn't that purty? Them cops sure had that town fixed up right nice. That's the way it's got to be all the way. Everybody settle down now peaceable-like." He tossed the grenade into the air again. Then, grinning, he looked over at Marshall and said, "That's what got you scared, ain't it? Some *he*-ro. Now, I got the guts to take the ride with this thing if I got to, but yer nuthin' but a yellowbelly." His satisfaction with the way things were going had made him forget that he had intended to kill Marshall, but Marshall did not know this. He was still white and visibly shaken.

With a swift sidelong glance Marshall became aware of Julian and two disappointed and reproachful eyes, magnified by the spectacle lenses, regarding him, questioning him, trusting him and waiting for him to do something, increasing the extent of Marshall's bitterness and frustration to the point where it almost overcame his fear. He knew he wasn't out of the woods yet. The man with the pistol would remember. *Christ, all this hero stuff and all that crap the goddamn movies and TV kept feeding people. Bang! Bang! You're dead! A lightning hip draw, or the guy getting up after being punched, kicked, slugged, and knocking the baddies on their asses. What shit! So when it really happened you stood there shaking with the sweat pouring out from under your arms and wanting to pee in your pants.* The man with the gun and the grenade was in command. Marshall had noted that when he flipped it he always caught it so that one finger was at the loop of the pin already half pulled out. One twitch and the bomb would be armed.

9

Curiously the fantasy that was now
being entertained by Julian had no
beginning, no end, but only a middle.
In the fantasy the Bubble Gun became
the classic long-barreled Colt. He would
beat the baddie to the draw and save
Marshall and all the rest.

The thought was clouding his
bewilderment over Marshall's strange
behavior. Julian had no way of realizing
the vast gulf between the dreamworld
of the idiot box in which puffs of smoke
issued from six-shooters and rifles but
somehow the good guys never seemed
to get hit except one or two expendable
extras, and the extraordinary cruelty of
reality in which lived people, good, bad
and indifferent, innocent and guilty,

who suddenly found themselves torn and shredded, dead or suffering excruciatingly. He had no measuring stick as to the speed with which a tragic situation can explode from static quiet into the most monstrous horrors. Nor had he the slightest inkling of the mind of Wilks who, ill-favored though he seemed, spoke to the woman in the understandable language of reasonableness. "Why, I got kiddies of my own at home I wouldn't want to see no harm come to any more'n you would yours. I like kiddies and kiddies like me." Nobody had been hurt, there had been no violence and within that context Julian's scenario would work. Headline: BOY HERO SAVES HIJACKED BUS.

However, to reach this middle part, this fantasy, where this sweet and beautiful dream would be realized he had to get there and so Julian arose and stood in the aisle. Automatically, the black Colt came up and followed him, the muzzle at one end of an imaginary line and the boy's forehead at the other.

Wilks said, "Hey, where do you think yer goin', sonny?"

Julian said, "I want a drink."

Stiff with horror Marshall hissed, "Sit down."

Julian darted a swift glance at him and then looked quickly away for there was the same frightened man, something he had never seen before, a grownup in the grip of almost abject fear. But this was not at all the Marshall of his fantasy, his friend who had been looking after him and offered to be his big brother if he came to any trouble, the Marshall that he, Julian, was now going to repay by saving him. A curious reversal. Julian suddenly had become Marshall and the cowering Marshall was Julian.

Julian said, "B-b-but I'm thirsty."

The fear that Marshall had known for himself was nothing to what gripped him now as he expected to see the child killed before his eyes, the heavy bullet smashing his skull, blood and brains spattering the surroundings. Out of the corner of his mouth he said, "For Christ's sweet sakes, sit down, you little bastard. You want to get us all killed?" But he was careful not to move. There was no telling what could light the fuse to that filthy, unstable package of maniacal explosive up front there.

As it happened, it was the self-adulation–self-pity syndrome that took over at that moment. Wilks sneered, "Well now, mister, that ain't no way to talk 'cause the little feller wants a drink."

A kind of blind anger suddenly replaced Marshall's fear of what Wilks might do and he lost his common sense. He said, "You're just looking for an excuse to kill someone, aren't you?"

It did seem that the more one accused Wilks of villainy, the more eager he became to exhibit the sweet moderation that lay behind the deadly weapons he wielded, and he whined, "Now, now, you folks got me all wrong," and then addressed Julian directly, "Young feller, don't you pay no mind to that yellowbelly. You just go and get yourself a drink."

And so there it was, things as they were actually happening, and the words out of the man's mouth, and nothing really of which to be frightened.

Politely Julian said, "Thanks," turned and marched

down to the water cooler where he pulled a paper cup out of the dispenser and, with his eyes watching Wilks and the whole frozen, static scene over the rim of his spectacles, took a long sip. The water cooler was just outside the door of the lavatory. Julian asked, "Can I g-g-go in here a minute?"

The kink of Wilks' mind now suddenly led away from death and down the path to comedy and he laughed, "Sure, sure, kid. When you gotta go, you gotta go. Ain't that right?"

Julian studied Wilks for a moment and then glanced again briefly at Marshall who was still sitting stiff and immovable, staring straight ahead, that Marshall who was a stranger to him. He went into the lavatory and shut the door behind him carrying his cup of water.

Inside the lavatory Julian was now firmly in the grip of how it seemed to him things could go, and, using a piece of the scented soap from the wash basin, he did what was necessary to implement the big and glorious dream.

And all the while the bus was rolling down the road to Mexico with its weird escort of armed and helpless outriders front and rear and two more helicopters from the Army raising dust overhead. Fields, fences, adobe houses, staring cattle flashed by. In city rooms far and near, wires were humming and early-edition stories were being written about the first hijacking of a transcontinental bus.

The momentary euphoria of his joke still had Wilks in its grip and he shouted to Milo Balzare, the little black-haired foreign musician, "Hey you, why don't you play some music to cheer the folks up like before. That was right nice." He waved the .45 in his direction. "You heard me."

Music was indeed all that was lacking in that weird, unbelievable scene. Balzare took up his hurdy-gurdy, touched the strings with his dark head bent over it for a moment and then picked out a slow, meditative and melancholy tune with the drone underlining the strangely repetitive sequence of the two interwoven melodies. None but he knew that he was playing *Pavane for a Dead Princess* by Ravel.

Wilks said, "What the hell kind of music do you call that? C'mon, give us some of that stuff like before."

Balzare, his eyes half closed from the effect of his playing but his face utterly composed, said evenly, "If I am to die this is the kind of music I choose to die to," and as though to emphasize his defiance he stepped up the *forte* of the drone and the melancholy melody rang through the bus more loudly as the door to the lavatory opened and Julian emerged, no longer carrying his paper cup but with his right hand in his jacket pocket.

Wilks turned his attention to him and asked, "Feel better, kid?"

The way he talked made it somehow so much simpler to go on. Julian said, "Uh huh. Thanks. Say, would you like to see my Bubble Gun I invented?"

Wilks queried, "Your what?"

At that moment Julian was level with Marshall, and Marshall noting Julian's hand tucked into his jacket pocket had a frightful prevision of what was coming and what the results could be, and could only breathe in anguish, "Oh God, no, Julian, don't."

But there was no Marshall for Julian then, only his own line to be followed, and he moved past him and produced his Bubble Gun.

In miniature it was almost an exact replica of the big Army cannon which for the moment had been held loosely but had now stiffened in Wilks' hand and was again leveled at Julian's freckled forehead, topped by his tousled carroty hair, and Wilks shouted, "Hey!" and for that instant there was the smell of death filling the bus, though Julian was unaware of it as he pulled the trigger of the only existing model of the Bubble Gun. A large iridescent soapy sphere blossomed from the muzzle, detached itself, floated away, caught a splinter of reflected light which turned it first gold, then blue and pink, after which it vanished in mid-air leaving a single drop to fall into the aisle.

The anticlimax was as much of a shock to all the passengers held in the thrall of terror as it was to the terrorist, as though the bubble had exploded with the roar of the hand grenade in the man's hand. Somebody laughed hysterically and Wilks, lowering his own gun, said, "Well, whaddya know. You say you invented that? C'mon up here and lemme have a look at it."

Julian said, "Yes sir," pulled the trigger again and produced a second bubble. This one chose to sail off in another direction to burst upon the pocket chess board held between the pair of chess fiends, causing them to look up angrily as it left a small damp spot.

Wilks said, "Well now, ain't that purty. But shucks, sonny, that's nuthin' but a l'il old water pistol."

Julian continued down the aisle protesting, "It's not a

water p-p-pistol. It's my Bubble Gun. I did so invent it.
I'm g-g-going to get a p-p-patent for it."

Wilks said, "Go on now. I don't believe it. You show
me." How he was enjoying the kindly, paternal figure he
was cutting behind his control of the situation and the
ever present threat of his weapons! They could all see
that Sam Wilks was a human being just like everybody
else and loved children. He let the big .45 hang loosely
from his trigger finger and held out his hand. "Let's have
a look."

Close to him now Julian raised his Bubble Gun,
pointed it into the face of Wilks and pulled the trigger
for the third time and here that middle part of the fantasy
which had no real start or finish did come to an end.
Reality, but of an unexpected nature, took over.

Instead of the fat, soapy sphere ballooning from the
muzzle there came a stream squirt, a succession of
small bubbles like a flight of colored bees and indeed
which, like such a swarm, suddenly enveloped Wilks'
face, bubbles pouring seemingly endlessly like rounds
from a machine gun, momentarily blinding him. He
yelled, "Oh, my eyes, my eyes. I'll kill . . . kill . . ." but
that was as far as he got even though by reflex he raised
both gun and grenade, but for that instant there was
nothing for him to see to shoot. That momentary distraction of the hijacker was all the bus driver needed.
He was ready with the big wrench that he had managed
to sneak to his side. He had it in his hand as he leaped
up from his seat, leaned over and with a backhand
stroke hit Wilks with all his force on the side of the
head and, even as the hijacker began to fall forward on

his face, the driver trod on the brake and jerked the bus to a halt.

And so for the end to Julian's fantasy it was still Marshall who saved the situation, for as Wilks began to topple forward, the ex-soldier saw that the finger looped in the grenade pin had reacted and pulled it loose. He had ten seconds. He needed only seven of them to whip out of his seat and flash down the aisle, knocking Julian out of the way, to dive, scrabbling frantically under the unconscious Wilks, and come up with the grenade in his hand, half sitting on the floor, one leg twisted under him almost in the position of a shortstop knocked off his feet by a hard-hit grounder. The driver's head was fortunately out of the way as he came on with his wrench for a second blow if it was needed. His window, the only one in the bus which was workable, was open. With all his force, Marshall, from his sitting position, flung the grenade. It sailed through the opening, over a farmer's fence and into a cabbage patch, where with a shattering roar it sent up a tremendous geyser of earth, knocking two state troopers off their motorcycles. Pieces of metal rattled against the side of the bus and starred one of the shatterproof windows. A shower of dirt and cabbage leaves descended. One of the overhead helicopters bucked like a mustang from the blast but was fought back into control. And then it was over.

Thereafter, for the first few minutes until rangers and state troopers regained control, there was the ugliest and most dangerous kind of chaos and hysteria, a melee of arms and legs within the bus, the sounds of heavy breathing, blows, the screaming of the women—and all in a

swirl of dust invading the interior from a landing helicopter.

It was dangerous without too, with the copters dis-
gorging armed men, others milling about, their fingers
on the triggers of rifles, pistols and automatic weapons,
knowing little, identifying no one, but jangled nerve
ends ready for messages to shoot.

At the front, piled up and writhing in the aisle of the
bus, was a heap of humans-into-animals, blindly and in-
sanely trying to hammer at the prone figure of the unconscious hijacker, shouting curses at him, losing all
sense of coordination, striking one another, flailing,
tearing, scratching. As the lawmen crowded in, blocking,
pushing and jostling one another at the narrow doorway,
their weapons at cock, the danger was far from over.

At the bottom of the heap, Marshall was covering
Julian with his body and at the same time trying to protect his own head and neck with his arms while shouting,
"Alright, alright, it's over! Get off! It's over! Stop it, stop
it!"

There had been just one remaining moment before
the wave of hysterical passengers engulfed him and
Julian for him to pluck Wilks' .45 from his fingers and
fling it away under a seat for he knew that anybody
caught with that weapon in his hand during the first
confused moments was likely instantly to be shot.

The dust swirled thicker as a third helicopter, this one
bearing press, touched down; someone outside let off a
rifle by accident and the crack of the shot brought about
one of those curious moments of stunned total silence
while the forces of hysteria gathered themselves anew.

But now there were new, savage voices to be heard, and thumps of blows, cries of pain and orders—"Okay, okay, break it up, break it up . . . Where is he?"

One by one, some half stunned, the men trying to get at Wilks were beaten and dragged off the heap and flung away down the aisle. The weight lifted and Marshall risking a glance upwards saw two massive leather-booted legs and a rifle butt about to descend upon him.

He yelled up, "Hey, wait! I got a kid under me!"

The steel edge stopped an inch from his skull and the big trooper said, "Git up and git your hands up . . ."

Marshall climbed slowly to his knees, his hands raised, careful to make no sudden movement. Beneath him Julian stirred, his clothing rumpled, his glasses knocked awry, his expression still dazed.

Then it was fortunate that the driver took a hand, his voice pitched high with still present hysteria. He pointed to the now revealed figure of Wilks, prone and motionless on his face. "There he is! That's the guy! That's the son of a bitch. The kid squirted something in his face and I let him have it with this."

The trooper glanced from the prone figure, to Marshall kneeling, to Julian trying to pull himself together and adjust his spectacles and finally to the driver standing there with the heavy wrench.

"I hit him with this," the driver repeated and showed the wrench.

Marshall said, "You'll find his gun under that seat."

The trooper kept his head and began to get a glimmer of what might have happened. He rolled Wilks over, took one look at him and said to Marshall, "Sorry! Okay, brother. Take care of the kid." Other troopers joined him and the first one shouted, "Okay, okay, everybody quiet down. We've got the guy." One of the others snapped cuffs onto Wilks' wrists and two more dragged him erect. A third peered into his face and said, "Say, this bastard's wanted. They just sent over a description of the guy who shot that filling station attendant at Carlsbad. A woman saw him from a window but was scared to report it . . ."

The swift, smooth action turned the chaos into the more orderly pandemonium of everyone trying to tell how it had happened:

"He was gonna blow us all up!"

"He aimed his pistol at my baby!"

"The kid! It was the kid shot him with a water pistol!"

"No, it was a gas gun!"

"The driver's a hero. The driver saved us all!"

Marshall picked Julian up, got him onto his knees beside him, brushed him off and helped him rearrange himself. He said, "Sorry if I was a bit rough, but . . ." He noticed then that the boy still had the little black pistol in his fist and said quickly, "Put that thing away in your pocket!" and helped him stow it. It seemed to him not a good time for anyone but the police to be seen having anything resembling a gun. But then to his surprise he found himself saying, "If anybody asks, say it was a water pistol. It makes it even better, see? You want to keep it secret until it's patented, don't you?"

Julian shook himself a little like a dog just out of water and said, "You got the grenade, didn't you?" All the fears and fantasies had evaporated. Reality was big brother Marshall who in the nick of time had grabbed the grenade and saved them all.

Marshall said, "Uh huh. Listen, what was all that about, you and those bubbles?"

There was no way Julian could tell him about how and what he had felt or about his imaginings so he said, "I loaded my B-B-Bubble Gun when I was in the you-know. There was some soap in there. I thought . . ." He trailed off and didn't finish the sentence.

Marshall looked at the child sharply. "You thought what?"

"I dunno. Well, maybe if he saw the bubbles he'd forget about shooting anybody. He was sort of crazy in the head, wasn't he?"

In all the hubbub swirling around them, the two seemed to be unnoticed kneeling together there, an is-land, isolated. Marshall studied Julian again. How much did children know and how could you tell? Had Julian tried to distract the killer without a thought as to what might happen to himself? Or had it been all just another scene reenacted out of some television western—*Bang, bang, you're dead*?

Julian suddenly seemed to levitate. A passenger had discovered him, seized him by the elbows and hoisted him up shoulder-high, shouting, "Hey, everybody, if you want to know who the real hero is, here he is!"

A reporter who had managed to squeeze into the bus queried, "Who? Where? What did he do?"

Julian looked down to Marshall for help but the latter only grinned up at him, "You're gonna be a hero, kid. Don't forget it was a water pistol."

There were plenty to give testimony:

"Bravest thing I ever saw. Walked right up to that murderer and squirted stuff in his eyes. He coulda been killed."

"What was it, some kind of gas gun?"

"Picked up the grenade and threw it out the window."

"Gave the driver the chance to conk him."

"What's your name, sonny? You ought to get a reward."

There was a diversion as the troopers called for a momentary emptying of the bus with, "Everybody out, please. Just for a moment. Let's get this bus cleared."

The confusion that had been within was nothing to what developed by the side of the road, with sheriff's men, rangers, state troopers, Army officers, copter pilots, excited passengers and reporters milling about while to the north and south, a king-size traffic jam of cars, small pickups and huge trailer trucks built up, leaning on their horns, or abandoning their vehicles to see what all the excitement was about.

The rangers had herded the passengers into a neighboring field along with the reporters in an attempt to sort out what had happened and interrogate witnesses. Photographers and reporters had cornered Julian in one group, the driver and his wrench which he never let go in another. Marshall hovered about the fringe keeping an eye on Julian. Nobody seemed to connect him with the episode of the grenade in all the excitement, which suited Marshall who did not like cops or newspapermen. Not one of two dozen eyewitnesses was going to get the story right anyway. Marshall was still considerably shaken by what he had been through, the narrowness of his escape, the escape of all of them, but what was taking precedence in his thoughts was the little black gun in the boy's hand, which in obedience to Marshall's instruction he was describing as an ordinary toy water pistol.

What had Marshall winging was all the palaver and the odd things that had happened before: the kid showing his diagram of what he claimed was his invention of a Bubble Gun, the Colonel of Ordnance taking it seriously, some kind of cloak-and-dagger crumb photographing it and then during the crisis, the kid coolly walking up the aisle, pulling the trigger and producing —soap bubbles. The goddamn thing worked.

The driver was posing for another picture and saying for the ninth time, ". . . So when he started yelling about his eyes, I seen my chance and let him have it with this . . ."

The bulk of the reporters and cameramen had Julian ringed.

"What did you say your name was, sonny?"

Marshall had meant to warn him not to give his right name—Smith, Jones, Brown, even Marshall. Within him was the heartbreak certainty that here was the finish of the boy's odyssey.

"Julian West."

"Where do you live?"

"S-S-San Diego, C-C-California."

"Traveling all by yourself?"

Julian did not see Marshall making frantic signals on the edge of the crowd and pointing to himself. "Uh huh."

"Where were you going?"

It was Marshall who spoke up quickly to answer that one, "He was going to Washington to visit his grandmother . . ."

"Tell us again how it all happened!"

Julian knew that for good form his reply should have been, "Aw, it was nothing; I just did what anybody would have done." But within himself he was quite well aware that it had *not* been "nothing," that something really tremendous had taken place which he did not understand at all, except that for a little he had not been Julian, but somebody else moving somehow through the dream of yet a third person, Marshall's perhaps. And so he remained silent and did not reply.

During the interviewing, two intelligent-looking, smartly dressed state troopers, sergeants both, had emerged from their black-and-white radio car and stood by watching and listening. One finally nodded to the other and said, "That's the boy, Buck."

The other watched and listened for another moment and then said, "I think you got something, Rick," and then to the crowd as he pushed forward with his companion, "Okay, okay, break it up. That's enough. You got the story."

They towered over Julian. Marshall could not understand the extent of the slightly sickish feeling that gripped him—*There goes Julian.*

The trooper named Buck bent down and said gently enough, "I think maybe your daddy would like to know where you are, wouldn't he?"

Julian looked up at him miserably. Marshall turned and walked away.

One would have said that Aldrin and Ellen West had been turned to stone, sitting there endlessly by the telephone, staring at it and waiting for it to ring with their anguished and haunted eyes, rather than their ears. There is no hell greater than the pictures limned by the imagination of the fate of a lost or stolen child.

When the telephone at last delivered its signal, it took West three rings before he could unfreeze to seize it by its throat, fumble the receiver and face the news, good or bad.

He said, "Hullo! Yes yes West speaking. You say you've got him . . . ?" He turned to his wife, "Mother, Mother, they've found him. They've got him." The voice was still coming from the receiver and West turned back to the phone, "Sorry, Lieutenant, I didn't get that. You say you're in touch with a radio car in . . . ? Where did you say? New Mexico? What, what? On a bus . . . ? A hero . . . ? Shot a hijacker . . . ?"

It was too insane and unbelievable, but the voice of the police Lieutenant at the other end was firm. West shouted to Ellen, "He's a hero. Shot a hijacker or something. And he's okay. Yes yes, go on, Lieutenant . . . He's right there at the radio car. Oh, thank God—Ellen, do you hear?"

She began to cry. "Please, Aldrin, I want him back. Tell them I want him back . . ."

The excited words came tumbling from West. "Listen, Lieutenant, can you . . . can they send him home? Sure, sure, the fastest way . . . anything . . . I'll pay transportation, charter a plane or whatever. Thank you, thank you, Lieutenant. And you'll keep us posted, won't you? We'll be right here."

He hung up nearly sick with relief, but when he turned to his wife again there was a puzzled frown building. "What did they mean he shot him with a water pistol; you can't shoot anybody with a water pistol. My God, Ellen, it must have been his Bubble Gun . . ."

They were over by the radio car—the two troopers, Julian and, within, the radio operator wearing a headset and working a powerful unit. The operator removed an earphone and spoke to the trooper named Rick who relayed the message on to Julian: "They've just been on to your home in San Diego, and I guess your ma was plenty worried about you. Now you just wait here a minute 'til we get this road cleared and we'll have you started home in a jiffy."

The trooper had unwittingly edited the message of West's concern and his offer to pay for a charter plane. Thus Julian's vivid imagination could picture his mother, but not at the moment his father. He supposed his father would laugh at him again when he got him home and probably take his Bubble Gun away as punishment.

A tall sheriff came up to the car and drawled, "Looka here, Sarge, if we don't get this road opened up . . . Mebbe you fellers better take charge . . ."

Buck said, "Yeah, okay," and to Julian, "Stick around, we'll be back," and to the operator, "Keep an eye on him, Jim."

In the neighboring fields, the situation had calmed down somewhat, though there were some excited knots discussing the event, with the driver still demonstrating his backhand technique with the wrench and one particularly voluble group of constabulary, state troopers, sheriffs and FBI men arguing over jurisdiction of the prisoner, now conscious and sullen, as to who was to take him in, where the hijacking had actually taken place, where begun, where ended and what state lines had been crossed.

The press, satisfied and eager to get to a wire and photo labs, had retired to their helicopter, as had the Army, which had no more interest in the affair. All three helicopters rose from the fields almost simultaneously, their rotors beating up a fog that for a few moments caused the entire neighborhood to vanish in a choking cloud of brown dust which shut off visibility.

When it cleared Julian was no longer beside the radio car. The operator wondered whether he ought to notify Buck, but just then a bleep from his set called him. He figured the kid wouldn't have got very far anyway.

Julian hadn't. He was just a small piece down the road fighting back tears of anger, and kicking viciously at the dry weeds at the side of the highway.

Marshall appeared out of the settling dust, brushing himself and muttering, "Christ, those bastards don't care if they choke you to death." He saw Julian. "Hey kid, you alright? What's the matter with you? Don't you know you're a hero—picture in the papers. Don't fold up now."

Julian took another savage kick at a tumbleweed. "The p-p-police!"

"What about the police?"

"They've talked with Dad. They say I've got to go home. I d-d-don't w-w-want to go home. I want to patent my Bubble Gun. What does Dad care?"

Marshall nodded. He had just wanted to be sure. He said, "Yeah, I know." He was thinking hard. "Sure, your Bubble Gun. I understand." He patted Julian's shoulder absently for a moment and then said, "Let's see that thing again."

Gloomily Julian fished into his pocket and handed him the Bubble Gun. No one was paying any attention to them. They were surrounded by a madhouse of arm-waving, whistle-blowing police and troopers, men shouting and cursing, motors revving up, giant trucks roaring their engines and over all the still settling dust of the copters.

Reflectively, Marshall played catch with the little gun, squinting down the muzzle and then, aiming it at nothing in particular, pressed the trigger. A single bubble emerged, detached and floated away into the air. By a curious refraction of the sun piercing the last remains of the dust whirled up by the aircraft, the bubble turned to pure gold and for a moment shone in the air like a little sun. It was borne aloft on a wave of hot air, seemed to twinkle at them for an instant and then, plop, it was gone.

Marshall gave the Bubble Gun another flip, caught it by the muzzle, looked down at the unhappy boy and said, "You wanna get to Washington?"

Julian could only nod assent. He didn't want to burst into tears before this man and if he had spoken all his pent-up misery might have let go.

Marshall said, "Okay. We go to Washington. You just trust your Uncle Frank, keep your mouth shut, your nose clean and do as I say. Here, put this away," and he stowed the Bubble Gun back into the boy's pocket. He took Julian by the hand and said, "See? We're just out for a nice little walk, you and I, so don't get jumpy."

They strolled casually through the pandemonium past assorted lawmen, past the bus with its passengers who under the direction of the driver were beginning to return to their places, past the black-and-white radio car.

Marshall said, "Just like that! Now we've gotta have maybe a little bit of luck."

They walked on down the line of still stalled northbound traffic, past cars and transport vehicles. Passing the latter Marshall merely glanced up into the cabs at the drivers and then walked on until he came to a huge double job, truck and trailer, canvas-covered. The pilot of this one was young, tough looking, short haired and bored. He was leaning on his elbow at the window in an attitude of *Okay, so I can stay here all day.* On the side of his cab was a sign, NO RIDERS.

Marshall said, "How 'bout giving us a lift, Mac? Me and my kid brother got to get to Albuquerque."

The driver looked them over lazily and said, "What's goin' on up front there?"

Marshall replied, "I dunno. They caught some crook hijacking a bus. Big deal. Look, if you're going through Albuquerque, our old lady's took sick and we're tryin' to get there."

The driver said, "Yeah?" and with one finger tapped the NO RIDERS sign.

Marshall said, "I saw that. Looks good." And then said, "You been overseas."

The driver nodded, "Uh huh."

"Where?"

The driver looked more interested and replied, "Ben Hoa. Thirty-first Carriers," to which Marshall said, "Oh, brother."

The driver queried, "You?"

Marshall replied, "An Loc. But you guys really caught it."

The driver nodded, "You said it. Okay, get in. I go through Albuquerque."

Marshall took a fast look around to see if anyone was noticing. No one was. They quickly climbed up into the cab of the truck, Julian squeezed between Marshall and the driver. From up front came the shrilling of more police whistles and the hot sound of engines starting up all along the way. The line was about to move.

Julian was in a state of pure bliss. He was with Marshall, he was free of police, a new adventure was beginning.

Marshall was figuring that the cops would be notifying the bus driver that the boy was being sent home. And this was exactly what was happening at that moment. As for himself turning up missing, Marshall thought, with six passengers lost off the trip, a seventh would be accepted by the driver as fate.

Slowly the file began to move, the truck joined the crawl.

Marshall said to Julian, "Your shoelace is untied."

Julian looked down at his feet. It wasn't. Before he could protest Marshall snapped, "You heard what I said," but managed to tip him a wink. "Christ, it's hot," he said, removing his jacket and holding it in his lap as Julian bent down, carefully untied both laces and then tied them again. The young driver was staring stonily ahead, his eyes on the tailgate of the truck preceding him. Traffic was beginning to speed up in both directions and the next moment they were passing the scene of the action with troopers waving the vehicles through.

One glimpse showed Marshall all he needed to see, the bus loaded and ready to take to the road again, the black-and-white radio car parked in the field now surrounded by troopers, agitatedly arguing. Marshall quickly turned his face away from the troopers and towards the truck driver and said, "That musta been where it happened. They sure got a lot of law around."

The driver turned and looked squarely at Marshall and said, "I don't go much for cops," and then they were past, rolling up the road at thirty, and as traffic spaced even more, up to fifty and every turn of the wheels put distance between them and those left behind.

Marshall apostrophized himself. *Well, you stupid bastard, if this isn't the craziest caper! But we're on our way.*

Back in San Diego, Lieutenant King of the Missing Persons Bureau, not too ably supported by Sergeant Cassidy, was going through one of the most unhappy and uncomfortable moments of his life trying to explain to a man with a thundering temper and a woman on the verge of screaming hysterics. It seemed he could get no further than, ". . . I'm afraid, sir, for the moment we just don't exactly know. Those hicks down there in Morellos fouled things up. We're in touch with them every minute. See, they had it all set up and then suddenly they said the kid was gone and . . ." and thereupon the storm burst over his battered head again. "Gone where? Gone why?

Who was in charge? Call the Police Commissioner, get through to the Governor." Words, shouts, threats, but nothing took away from the fact that Julian and his Bubble Gun had vanished into the blue again.

During a part of that night Julian was asleep, his head on Marshall's lap. The truck driver said, "Your old lady's took sick bad, eh?"

Marshall was drowsy and momentarily off guard. He said, "What? Whose old lady?"

The truck driver never took his eyes off the road through which his blazing headlamps were boring a tunnel but his voice had an edge as he said, "Yours—and the kid's, too, if he's your brother."

Marshall tried to cover. He said, "Oh, sure, sure. I'm afraid she don't have much longer to go. She's gettin' on."

The driver said, "Look here, feller, this isn't any kind of a caper, is it?"

Marshall said, "No, it isn't."

The truck driver regarded the handsome profile for a moment in the dim lighting from the dashboard and said, "Okay then. We ought to be in Albuquerque in the morning and if it's any kind of a racket I'm gonna turn you in."

The big truck was on schedule and at eight A.M. drew up at an intersection in the heart of the business area of Albuquerque. A policeman was directing traffic, passersby were stopping at a corner newsstand to reduce piles of morning papers with black, blazoning headlines and pictures.

The driver said, "Albuquerque. All out."

Marshall reached over a hand and said, "Thanks, friend."

The driver ignored the gesture and said, "Okay, bud, and watch out for the cops."

"What cops?"

The driver snorted. "While you were sacked out last night I heard it on the radio. There's a five-state alarm out for your kid brother. You said this wasn't a caper."

Marshall said, "I swear it isn't."

The driver said, "You're a great kidder, ain't you? You better give. You know I'm not supposed to pick anybody up. I could lose my job. You see that cop over there? I bet he'd like to know."

Marshall said, "Okay, pal, but just hang onto that kid a sec." He jumped down from the cab, grabbed a copy of the morning paper, left two bits and was back in again handing it to the driver. "Here, read this."

The man stared at the hijacking headlines and photographs and took in the early text with bulging eyes and then said, "Well, for Pete's sake. This the kid?"

Marshall said to Julian, "Show him."

Julian produced the Bubble Gun and squeezed the trigger. It was on its machine-gun kick, releasing first a whole flight of colored bubbles and then one large juicy one which changed magnificently into every shade of the rainbow before bursting upon the edge of the cab window.

The driver goggled and managed to get out, "Well, whaddya know? Brother!" but then said swiftly to Marshall, "So, where do you come in?"

It was Julian who filled in the gap. "He's my friend.

He's helping me. I'm g-g-going to Washington to patent it and m-m-make a lot of money. They're t-t-trying to stop me."

Marshall said, "I'm giving the kid a hand. Wouldn't you?"

The driver's face broke into a grin. He said, "Okay then, good luck. Beat it, and keep your eyes peeled. Get out on this side and the cop won't notice."

They shook hands and Marshall and Julian slipped from the offside of the cab. The driver crashed into gear, wheeled his truck around the corner and left the two standing on the busy intersection feeling naked.

Marshall had to take a chance. He said to the news vendor, "Excuse me, Mac, where's the bus station?"

The man was busy making change and didn't even look up. He said, "Straight ahead, four blocks. You can't miss it."

Marshall looked in the direction indicated. There was the traffic cop at the intersection and two blocks down a prowl car was parked at the curb. Marshall cursed himself. There were now several reasons why he wanted to finish what he had started. If they picked up the kid, he would, of course, be sent home immediately but Marshall was uncertain as to what charges would be brought against himself. He took Julian by the hand, keeping him on the inside away from the curb and when the lights and the wave of the traffic cop's arm were with them, they crossed the intersection. The cop was too busy keeping the early morning business bustle moving to pay them any mind. But the prowl car with its radio! And passersby too, one out of every three of whom must have heard the alarm on the morning news for the red-haired kid with the cheaters and the stammer. Oh Christ! Was there any way around to get to the bus station another way? There they were, Julian still carrying his small case, Marshall's belongings in one slightly larger. They were as conspicuous as though they had been bearing placards announcing their identity.

Marshall noticed suddenly that they had halted opposite a facade and entrance to one of the larger branches of the J. C. Penney chain of stores a half block in length. Marshall gave vent to an exclamation, "C'mon, kid," and, instead of going on, turned and with Julian entered the store.

The two CIA men had managed to elude the guards and officials at the gate leading to the tarmacs and runways of Mexico City's International Airport not far from where the Russian giant four-engine Tupelov jet aircraft was waiting. All the passengers had been herded inside, but the boarding steps had not yet been removed. The two men were watching the entrance anxiously.

The first said, "You sure he wasn't among the passengers?"

The other, consulting a photograph, said, "They wouldn't be that dumb."

"Disguised maybe?"

"That isn't how they operate."

"They're obviously waiting for him."

"Uh huh."

The first CIA man sighed and said, "Well, here we are. There's the guy. That's the little bastard who stole the shot."

Nikolas Allon emerged from the departure building. He was surrounded fore and aft and on both sides by six large, tough-looking and obviously well-armed Russian bodyguards.

The second CIA man groaned, "And his pals."

The first operative said, "Jesus, there'll be hell to pay if we don't stop him. They're going crazy in Washington."

"They go crazy. We're the patsies. What do we do?"

They both had their hands inside their jackets fingering the butts of their shoulder-holstered guns only to find themselves hypnotized by the slow methodical march of the group striding across the tarmac in the direction of the plane. The bodyguards were looking about them and in every direction. If they noted the two CIA men when they came within range of the standing pair, they gave no sign. The hands of the two emerged from their jackets—empty.

The second CIA man put it succinctly, saying "Kamikazes we ain't."

Allon climbed the stairs and entered the aircraft. The bodyguard remained grouped below until he had vanished inside the ship and the heavy door slid shut. Attendants pulled away the boarding stairs, others removed the chocks from the wheels. The four jet engines breathed heavily, setting up miniature whirlwinds of dust and papers. The plane moved away and soon was heading down the runway for the takeoff point. Thereafter the two men watched the great tin bird heave itself into the deep blue Mexican sky where for an instant its glittering silver was framed against the white of the snow on the peak of Popocatepetl.

The second CIA man murmured softly, "Next stop, Moscow."

His partner spat in disgust, "Operation Balls!"

The second CIA man supplied the coda, "You can't win 'em all, chum."

Marshall and Julian emerged from the glass portal of J. C. Penney. Marshall was clad in a different shirt, his stripped-down battle jacket had been stowed away and was replaced by a brown and white leather windbreaker of unborn calfskin. On the back of his head he wore a tan cowpuncher's ten-gallon hat.

But the greatest transformation had been worked upon Julian, for he was now wearing a shirt with BUFFALO BILL lettered across the chest, fringed buckskin trousers and coat. His glasses had been removed and in addition he was wearing a Buffalo Bill Stetson. To complete the illusion, glued to his upper lip and chin was a Buffalo Bill moustache and goatee. He was carrying a toy rifle, and around his middle was a leather belt containing dummy cartridges and a pistol holster into which the Bubble Gun had been thrust. Minus his glasses, his carroty hair covered by the Stetson, plus the costume, the goatee and moustache, he was practically unrecognizable.

Marshall no longer felt nude. He looked down upon Julian with a wide grin and said, "How's that?"

Julian replied, "G-g-great. Is this what Buffalo B-B-Bill really looked like?"

"He sure did. You're the spittin' image. Okay, let's go." For he was now prepared to make the test.

They moved off. The cop at the intersection was still directing traffic, the patrol car containing two police was still there. Squatting on the sidewalk opposite the car was an old and wrinkled Indian surrounded by articles of Indianware, rugs, beads and phony turquoise jewelry. Marshall leaned down and whispered something into Julian's ear.

They approached the corner. Marshall said to Julian, "Get 'im, Buffalo."

Julian pointed the wooden rifle at the Indian and said, "B-b-bang, you're dead."

The Indian looked up, smiled a cheerful, toothless smile and held out a colorful woven basket. "Indian basket. Fi' dolla. Very cheap."

Julian drew another bead. "B-b-bang!"

They were level now with the prowl car. One of the cops leaned out of the window grinning and said, "Hey, there, don't you shoot old Pete. Him once great big Indian chief Thunder Face, eh, Pete?"

The Indian offered the basket again. "Four dolla."

Marshall winked at the policeman. "Old Buffalo Bill here, he just naturally shoots them pizen varmints on sight. C'mon Bill, you got 'im." They moved on.

The policemen in the car smiled as they went and said, "Kids." Marshall was satisfied.

They continued on threading their way through pedestrians.

Julian said, "Say, they r-r-really thought I was B-B-Buffalo Bill, didn't they?"

Marshall stopped dead so abruptly that Julian who was still holding his hand was almost yanked off his feet. "Listen kid, that goddamn stammer of yours."

The sudden change in Marshall's voice and expression was so startling that Julian looked up at him in alarm.

Marshall continued, "If anybody got suspicious of us that's the first thing they'd nail you on. Do you have to do it?"

Julian said, "I d-d-don't know."

"It's really a lot of crap, isn't it?"

Julian said, "I g-g-guess—I guess so—if you say." He was already half hypnotized by his worship and love for Marshall.

Marshall said, "Right. So, from now on we cut out the stammer. Let's hear you say Bubble Gun."

"Bubble Gun."

"That's great. Now say ding-dong-dell, pussy's in the goddamn well."

Julian repeated, "Ding-dong-dell, pussy's in . . ."

Marshall stopped him with a wave of his hand, "See, there you are. Who needs it?"

Julian said, "Okay," and then with the casualness of the child who is utterly finished with a subject that is not likely ever to come up again, went on to the next. "Where do we go now?"

"You still want to go to Washington, don't you?"

"Sure, what do we do?"

Marshall said, "Find the bus station. You've got your through ticket, haven't you?"

"Sure."

Marshall said, "Okay. They're good from anywhere. Let's go."

10

Innovation in crime, as both police and media know, invariably sparks imitators and as one gray head in a Los Angeles city room remarked in disgust, "Christ, a bus hijacked! Can you beat it? I suppose we'll have one a week now."

He did not have that long to wait, for the next alarm in the headquarters of the bus company at Oklahoma City came in exactly twenty-four hours later concerning Bus 150, Los Angeles to New York via Flagstaff, Albuquerque, Kansas City, St. Louis, Chicago and Cleveland, aboard which the Coote sisters were traveling on their first package tour of the United States. It was this alert pair that made the discovery that there was a hijacker aboard.

The Coote sisters, Vera and Prudence, were British, unmistakably so. Spinster sisters, habitat Vine Cottage, Birdsfeather Lane, Little Eggham, Dorset, they had been the first to notice the resemblance of the man slouched across the aisle from them to the hijacker of the San Diego bus whose portrait and the story of whose crime graced the front page of their copy of *The Los Angeles Times* and which they had been studying with delighted horror. They had been warned by both the Vicar and the Colonel back home of the dangers of travel, let alone life, in the Colonies, and here was breathtaking evil that in a way had touched them. Hijacking of a bus. *They* were on a bus.

The Coote sisters had devoured the story in the newspaper, the horrible menace to the passengers of death by gunfire, bomb, or both, the brave boy who had saved them all, the villainous perpetrator shown both shackled to the police and later arraigned. He looked every bit as bad as he was, dirty denim trousers, open shirt, curious leather jacket, and Stetson, his face smudged with a growth of beard, eyes bleary. He looked, in fact, just as wicked as did the fellow sitting opposite them in worn denims, open shirt, odd jacket patterned in brown and white fur, cowboy hat pulled down over his eyes, face bristling with two days' growth. In fact, Vera and Prudence admitted to one another with the first *frisson* of horror, the men looked very much alike. Perhaps all hijackers in the Americas wore a standard kind of uniform. Whatever, the sisters decided that the man would bear watching.

Prudence whispered, "Where did he get on?"

Vera replied, "I don't remember. He wasn't there last night."

"Do you think that the child is with him?"

Vera said, "I don't know."

The child was dressed in some kind of a playsuit and most of the time had been looking out the window. Neither he nor the potential hijacker had addressed each other.

The two nervous sisters gave themselves the thrill of reading the story all over again but rather ignored the brief short which appeared at the end under the heading POLICE SEEK MISSING BOY—YOUNG HERO VANISHES, and datelined El Paso, reading to the effect that the police had sent out a general alarm for Julian West, the young hero who had foiled the San Diego bus hijacking and who had apparently vanished from the scene shortly after the incident. The squib did not, of course, hint at the complete bafflement of the police. One moment, according to every officer interrogated, the boy had been sitting by the side of the road waiting for the troopers to clear the traffic jam before driving him to El Paso and a plane for home, and the next he wasn't there or anywhere else and since his disappearance no trace of him had been reported.

The bus was tooling along U.S. Highway One east of Albuquerque and entering the red and sand colored rocky wilderness of the Manzano Badlands.

Vera, in the window seat, looking out, observed, "What terrifying country! It's so different from Little Eggham, sometimes I wonder if we really should have come."

Prudence said, "Of course it's different, but that's why one travels."

"Supposing there are Indians? The Vicar said . . ."

"Don't be silly. The Vicar's a fool. They killed off all the Indians. And after that, the bootleggers. Though, I suppose the Colonies have never really been civilized."

Vera said, "Now, it's hijackers."

Prudence said, "I'm watching him," and stole another glance at the man slouched in his seat a few feet away from them.

In a bus that seemed filled with innocent enough and typical Americans on the move, businessmen, a few blacks, salesmen, ranchers, farmers, a family of mother, father, small son and daughter, an elderly woman going to visit her married children, he was the only really desperate-looking character.

The Vicar, of course, the Coote sisters were aware, was hopelessly behind the times, but their friend, the Colonel, a relic of World War One, the sisters had taken more seriously. The Colonel had read up and was something of an expert on American lawlessness, and when the two had come by a windfall inheritance and decided to see something of the world beginning with Britain's first colony to be given its independence, the Colonel had briefed them thoroughly on what might be expected, bringing them up to date on the various types of crime rampant in the States with the exception of that extra, added bonus which they were now encountering, the hijacking of a transcontinental bus.

Though there was five years difference between them, Prudence being the elder, there was not much to tell them apart. They had the same angularity, washed-out eyes, colorless hair and prominent teeth. They were both swathed in sensible tweeds of similar patterns and wore cloth hats.

"Oh," said Vera. "We're stopping. What do you suppose it is . . . ?"

Prudence looked to her right at a sign and said, "HUMBLE. What a funny name! Goodness, it's a petrol station. We're stopping for petrol."

Across the aisle, Julian asked, "Where's Humble?"

Marshall said, "Nowhere. It's a gas station." He barely glanced out of the window as the bus drew up to one of the big Western oil company's pumps. They seemed to be just outside a hamlet called Adamana. They had left New Mexico and now had crossed into Texas and the bus driver, fat, cheerful, perspiring, his shirt dark at the armpits, got out and walked over to the diesel pump and talked to the uniformed attendant. Although conversation could not be heard owing to the thick windows required by the air-conditioning system, a clattering from without did penetrate as a Texas state trooper on a motorcycle drew up, stopped, remained sitting on his bike, but engaged the driver and the attendant in conversation. Then, all three looked over in the direction of the bus.

Marshall said, "Oh, Christ. Duck."

Julian, alarmed, cried, "What's the matter?"

Marshall said, "Shut up and get down. The fuzz. He may have spotted us."

The policeman, the driver and the attendant were now looking directly into the window where they were sitting.

Julian obediently squidged down below window level, Marshall slid down in his seat as low as he could and pulled the brim of his hat over his eyes.

However, he had to know and out of the side of his mouth he said, "Julian . . . I mean, Buffalo."

The boy replied, "Yeah?"

"Take a quick peek. What are they doing? The cop, I mean?"

Julian popped up and down in the approved TV style and then said, "They're all talking and looking over here," and then he asked in a conspiratorial whisper, "Are they on our trail?"

Marshall replied, "I dunno, but keep down and don't look any more. Here, pretend like you're reading," and he shoved a comic book over at him.

Under his breath he said, "Oh, Christ, the goddamn bus driver," for there was no doubt in his mind that something was up. He had caught a glimpse of the driver talking and twitching his head in the direction of the bus and seen the trooper, risen from the saddle of his cycle, craning his neck and looking directly at him, Frank Marshall.

It was just the last half minute or so of this drama which the Coote sisters caught when Prudence happened to look to her right and saw the trooper craning his neck, staring, and its shattering effect upon the desperado across the aisle.

She seized her sister's arm and whispered, "Vera, did you see?"

"Yes."

"Do you suppose he recognized him?"

"Oh, Prudence, how terrifying!"

Prudence squeezed Vera's hand again, "Look at him. If that isn't the guilt of a hardened criminal."

Vera whispered, "Ssshhh. For heaven's sake, Prudence, be careful. He might hear you."

At this point the meeting at the diesel pump broke up, the driver lifted his hand in a gesture of goodbye and got back into the bus.

Prudence leaned closer to her sister, "Oh, dear, it doesn't seem as if he's going to do anything. The policeman, I mean."

Vera said, "Perhaps he didn't recognize him after all. But you would think that after having his picture in all the papers . . ."

Prudence said, "Don't be stupid. That's the other one. They caught *him*. Oh, dear, maybe he didn't see him."

The noise of the bus in full swing again was providing cover for the whispers of the two.

Vera said, "He's acting guilty."

"Not like an honest man."

"I shan't have another quiet moment."

Prudence now reached down and picked up her handbag, which was actually a rather oversized reticule and heavy, and placed it between her and Vera, remarking grimly, "I'm afraid the Colonel was right."

This was how fear came to four of the inmates of Bus 150. This was how it had looked to them from inside the bus. From the outside the conversation, unfortunately inaudible to the four within, was somewhat more innocent.

The state trooper had opened with, "Hello, Fatso."

The bus driver said, "Hi, Tex."

The attendant said, "How many gallons?"

Fatso replied, "Fill 'er. I don't like goin' over this stretch without I know I got plenty." He turned to the trooper and said, "Whaddya know, Tex."

Tex replied, "Nuthin'. What's with you?"

Fatso said, "Same old load," and then added, "No, I got a couple of Limeys aboard. Sisters. Real kooks. Can they ask questions!"

Tex said, "No kiddin'."

Fatso said, "One of 'em's got Indians on the brain. Are we gonna be attacked by Indians?"

Tex repeated, "No kiddin', where are they?"

Fatso motioned with his hand in the direction of the bus and said, "In the back there. You can just see their heads. They're on the other side."

Tex hoicked himself up off the seat of his motorcycle and craned his neck so that he could see better. The attendant stopped cranking the diesel pump and had a look for himself.

Tex asked, "Them two with the hats?"

Fatso said, "Yeah. Get a load."

Tex remarked, "It takes all kinds, don't it? English you said they was?"

"Uh huh. They talk like they got a hot potato in their kissers."

The attendant said, "Sixty-three gallons."

Fatso said, "Okay, charge it," and produced the bus line's credit card.

Tex was still standing looking over at the bus and suddenly found himself staring into four alarmed eyes as the heads of the two sisters were turned in his direction and staring back.

"Boy," he said, "they're a couple, ain't they? Indians!"

Fatso restored his credit card to his wallet, said thanks to the attendant and "So long, Tex, don't fall off your bike."

Tex said, "Okay, Fatso-boy, drive careful and watch out for Injuns."

Fatso got back into his bus, slammed the door shut, rolled her back onto the highway and they were off.

After a few moments Marshall side-mouthed, "Take a look out the back window. Is that cop following us?"

Julian got up, knelt on the seat and looked backwards to investigate. He said, "No, I can't see anyone." He withdrew his gun from its holster and aimed it through the back window and said, "If he comes I'll shoot him with my Bubble Gun." Marshall reached up in sudden panic and said, "Oh Christ, put that thing away, will you, and keep it away."

Julian regarded him reproachfully saying, "Okay, okay, I was only fooling," and then added, "Were you scared again?"

Marshall replied, "Not scared. Just careful. I'm trying to keep you from being grabbed. But even if he'd spotted you he wouldn't have recognized you in that outfit." He sat up in his seat again, shoved back his hat and mopped his brow.

Prudence Coote had gone quite stiff and now shifted her reticule and put it onto her lap.

She leaned to Vera, "Do you see? He's armed. I knew it."

"Prudence, I shall die."

"He's using the child as a decoy. We must do something at once."

"Oh please, Prudence, no. He would shoot us."

"Hush, he needn't know."

"What will you do?"

"Tell the driver at once."

Vera began to shake. "Oh Prudence, don't leave me. I shall die of fright."

Prudence ran the Union Jack up to the masthead over the ramparts and ordered the bugles to blow the charge. She said, "Vera, remember that we are British."

She rose, holding her bag for a moment, then on second thought placed it carefully in Vera's lap. "There," she said, "and don't hesitate." She moved off, carefully refraining from bestowing so much as a glance upon Marshall, who was now sitting up reading a comic book again, or Julian, whose nose was flattened against the window pane.

Her chin quivering with nervousness, Vera watched her sister, back ramrod-stiff, march down into the driver's well where she leaned over and whispered to him. She saw him stand up at his wheel and turn his fat baby face to look anxiously towards the back of the bus. There was some further whispering after which the driver nodded his head. Prudence came marching down the aisle again, all flags flying and a look of satisfaction upon her face. She sat down, retrieved her carry-all and placed it firmly upon her lap. Her eyes were turned towards the front end of the bus and she craned her neck slightly to see better.

Vera whispered, "Did you tell him?"

"Ssshhh!" cautioned Prudence. She elongated her neck another centimeter and then relaxed as she saw the driver pick up his microphone.

And thus the second hijack alarm came into the Oklahoma City Dispatcher's Office, where the operator listened to a hoarsely whispered message from Bus 150, Los Angeles to Washington, and then cried aloud, "What? Oh, for godssake, not again. Are you sure?"

His exclamation attracted the attention of the Chief Dispatcher who queried, "What's up?"

The dispatcher with a look of disbelief on his face said, "What the hell is going on here? Bus one five oh reports a suspicious character. Sounds like another hijacker. He's armed."

The Chief groaned, "I knew it, I knew it. There was bound to be another. Has he made his move yet?"

"The driver says not yet."

"Where are they?"

The operator waved for silence and then reported, "He says they're east of Tucumcari, through Glenrio and just before Vega. That's some pretty wild country. A passenger saw him take out a gun. He looks just like the other guy."

The Chief Dispatcher had already signaled his telephone switchboard, shouting, "Get me police headquarters," and then said to the man at the microphone, "Look, tell him to keep his shirt on and not to lose his nerve. Just pretend he doesn't know anything and keep on driving. Get it? We'll handle it. Get his exact position." To the telephonist he yelled, "Get me Captain Russell." The dispatcher queried the driver and then called to the Chief Dispatcher, who was already at the phone, "He's three miles east of Glenrio, doing sixty. He ought to be near Wildorado in twenty minutes."

The Chief Dispatcher said, "Hello, Russ? Keegan, Chief Dispatcher, Inter-State. Our driver on Bus one five oh, L.A. to Washington, reports there could be another hijack attempt. He just passed through Glenrio. Can you get a roadblock somewhere around Wildorado? He hasn't made his move yet."

11

The roadblock had been installed
efficiently and strategically around the
corner of a large left-hand bend so that
there was no chance of anyone in the
bus seeing it until the very last moment
when they came out of the turn where
the straightaway began again. The fat
driver, sweat pouring from him, sighed
with relief as he saw the barrier across
the highway, the police sign and the
roadside swarming with men. State
troopers and sheriff's cars, pistols,
shotguns and one submachine gun were
in evidence. A quick look into the
rear-vision mirror brought further relief
to the driver. None of his passengers
had stirred. He eased to a halt.

Looking forward towards what

appeared to be a small army, there was no longer any
doubt in Marshall's mind. He groaned, "Oh no! Son of
a bitch! And I figured we had got away clean. That goddamn cop back at the gas station and the driver giving
him the dope. Probably didn't want to tackle it alone so
he telephoned ahead."

He felt Julian's searching gaze upon him and knew that
the boy was looking to see whether he was scared. He
wasn't any longer. Nevertheless, he must give hope. He
said, "Remember, you're my kid brother and let me do
the talking."

Julian asked, "Do I keep my beard on?"

Marshall replied, "Yeah. And your hair too and
remember, no stammer. Wait a minute, put that gun in
your pocket—no, you better give it to me—hell, leave it
where it is." Marshall dropped his hand over the hol-
stered Bubble Gun so as to conceal it.

The Coote sisters saw him do it and exchanged
glances.

Vera asked, "Is he going to shoot?"

Prudence replied, "I don't think so. We're saved."

For at that moment the driver had swung the door
open and, with the bus entirely surrounded by armed
men, two burly sheriffs climbed aboard and positioned
themselves at the head of the gangway, huge florid West-
erners with hands like hams, but curiously innocent and
almost cherubic and childlike faces that belied the great
cannons slung from their hips. They needed no microphone and the leader of the two boomed forth.

"Folks, I'm Sheriff Casper of Navajo County here
speakin' to you and this is my deputy, Williams. Jes' to

say there ain't no need to git excited or upset-like. We're jes' carryin' out a little routine investigation for someone maybe the law is lookin' fer and we're askin' fer yer kind cooperation."

The phrase "someone maybe the law is looking for" was all the confirmation Marshall needed. He resorted to the side of his mouth again and said to Julian, "That's us. Play it cool."

Sheriff Casper was announcing, "Me and my deputy here will now pass down through the bus jes' askin' y'all to produce any identification you might have and if anyone is packin' any hardware, we'd appreciate it if you'd jes' be so kind as to hand it over butt end to."

The passengers stirred and rustled with unease and turned and looked about their immediate vicinity to see who the culprit or desperado might be who had brought out this army.

Sheriff Casper queried the first passenger on his right, "Yer identification, suh?"

The passenger said, "Harry Morrison. I'm a salesman. Bathroom fixtures. My car broke down at St. Elmo. Here's my social security card and driver's license."

"Much obliged, suh. You carryin'?"

Harry Morrison reached into his right hip pocket and produced a flat .38 automatic which he first carefully turned around, then tendered grip end first.

Sheriff Casper said, "That sho is a lotta gun."

Morrison said apologetically, "Well, when you do a lot of driving at night . . . Here's my license to carry."

The Sheriff said, "Sho, sho, cain't say I blame you. I'll jes' hang onto this fer a minute." And then, removing his ten-gallon hat, he dropped the gun into it and went on to the next passenger, a woman who handed him a driving license, "Mrs. J. R. McQuarey, 437 Elm Avenue, La Jolla, California."

"Very kind of you, ma'am."

Mrs. McQuarey explained, "I was just going to Oklahoma City to visit my mother. See, here's my ticket."

"Thank you, ma'am, I guess that tallies." The Sheriff indicated her handbag and said, "Now, what about that there little . . ."

With a slight flush of embarrassment she produced a small, pearl-handled, short-barreled .32. She said, "My husband . . ."

Sheriff Casper lifted an eyebrow. He said, "You ain't got nuthin' against yer husband now, have you, ma'am?"

"Oh, no, Sheriff, it's just that when I travel alone, he thinks I ought to . . ."

The Sheriff said, "Well, now, ma'am, maybe he's right. We'll just have it for a moment." He deposited it into his hat and moved on.

By the time the two had proceeded the length of the bus and approached Marshall, Julian and the Coote sisters, they had unearthed no one whose *bona fides* was not impeccable. On the other hand, Sheriff Casper's Stetson was now practically overflowing with weapons, pistols of every kind and caliber, including a .22 Woodsman, .32's, .45's both in automatic and revolver, an old-fashioned double-barreled gambler's derringer, one bowie and one hunting knife in an ornate sheath. Marshall was sitting quietly and looking both wary and puzzled. Were they after him and Julian and, if they were, why didn't they grab them immediately, and if they weren't what the hell was this all about?

Prudence had been watching the approach of the pair and suddenly turned to Vera and said, "Oh dear," but she recovered quickly when the two men arrived at their station. Casper glanced at Marshall, then at the Coote sisters, and Prudence summoning all her courage gave him an almost imperceptible nod of her head in Marshall's direction. The Sheriff exchanged glances with his deputy and then said to Marshall, "Okay, young feller, what's yer name?"

Looking up from beneath the brim of his hat, Marshall looked imperturbed, if anything, slightly derisive, "Frank Marshall."

"Identification?"

Marshall reached inside his shirt and pulled out dog tags which were attached to a thin chain. They clinked faintly as the Sheriff examined them.

The Sheriff nodded and said, "Oh, I see. How long you been back?"

"Fourteen months."

"Where you goin'?"

"Washington."

"What fer?"

"Guy promised me a job."

The Sheriff indicated Julian, "Who's he?"

"My kid brother."

"What's his name?"

Marshall said the first name that came into his head, "Herman."

Julian looked up startled.

The Sheriff said, "Herman, eh? Looks like Buffalo Bill to me." Then, to Marshall, "You heeled?"

"No."

"Any objection to a frisk?"

Some mockery had come into Marshall's voice as he replied, "Yes, but go ahead."

He stood up and raised his arms and Casper nodded to his deputy who gave Marshall a quick professional going-over.

Deputy Williams reported, "He's clean."

Marshall sat down again. As he did so, Prudence in a quick gesture pointed to Julian.

The Sheriff caught it and said to Julian, "Okay, Herman Buffalo Bill, let's have a look at that cannon."

Julian extracted the Bubble Gun from its holster and with the same care and grownup gesture he had seen adopted by the others handing over their weapons, he held it by the muzzle and handed the butt end to the Sheriff. He said, "Be careful."

The Sheriff asked, "Loaded, is it?"

Julian replied, "It isn't a real one. It's a Bub—"

Before he had finished the sentence, a hand dropped onto his leg, cutting him off.

Marshall said, "Oh, for godssake, Sheriff, it's a kid's toy."

The Sheriff gave it only a cursory examination, shook it once and then handed it back, saying, "Okay, Buffalo," and then to Marshall, "Sorry about the frisk, brother. No offense." He then turned to the two Coote sisters. "Well now, what about you two ladies here?"

Almost in unison, Prudence and Vera replied, "We're

British." And then Prudence added, "The Misses Vera and Prudence Coote, Vine Cottage, Birdsfeather Lane, Little Eggham, Dorset." She opened her reticule partly and then quickly closed it again, just sufficiently so that she was able to get her hand in to fumble and produce their two passports.

"We're on a tour," she said, handing them to Sheriff Casper.

He gave the passports a cursory glance and handed them back. "Well, now that's jes' fine and allow me to say that yer mighty welcome to our country."

"Course, you ladies wouldn't be packin' any shootin' irons." Deputy Williams said this not as a question but more like a statement of something highly obvious, but just as the Sheriff and Williams were about to turn away, they caught a glance of alarm exchanged between the two sisters.

The Sheriff altered his deputy's statement to a question. "No offense, ladies, but I guess we got to ask you like everybody else. Are you carryin' any lethal weapons?"

Prudence and Vera exchanged another look, this time of complete panic.

Vera turned to her sister and said, "I'm afraid you're going to have to, Pru."

Slowly, and looking up into Sheriff Casper's face with a mixture of fright and sheepishness, Prudence opened her huge reticule and extracted therefrom, held by the muzzle with great distaste and anxiety, an enormous British Army revolver of about 1892 vintage.

Deputy Williams took it from her. "Goshamighty, what

do you call that?" He handed the gun to Sheriff Casper.

Casper examined the gun and read off the maker's mark, "Webley, Mark III Army Issue, 1890," and then addressed Prudence, "Is it loaded, ma'am?"

Prudence looked terrified. "I don't know."

Sheriff Casper worked an ejector on the gun and five huge brass shells clinked into his hand.

Prudence gave a little shriek of alarm. "Oh, dear, is that what they look like?"

Sheriff Casper asked, "Ma'am, where'd y'all git a thing like this?"

Vera replied, "Our grandfather carried it in the Crimean War."

Prudence said, "Boer War, Vera, not Crimean."

"Grandfather always said it was the Crimean War," Vera protested.

"Come, Vera, you know grandfather was always a little dotty. It couldn't have been the Crimean. He was only a baby then."

"Oh, dear, I get so confused about our wars," Vera sighed, and then brightly and rather sweetly she said to Sheriff Casper, "We've had so many, you know."

Sheriff Casper returned to the point. "Well, now whatever do you ladies want to be carryin' a thing like this fer?"

Prudence replied, "You see, we were coming to America for the first time and the Colonel had warned us, well, you know, the dangers, and we thought we'd better . . ."

Sheriff Casper, in dead earnestness, said, "Why, ma'am, you don't need nuthin' like that over here. You're jes' as safe as you would be in yer own home. This is a peace-lovin' country."

He was moved by the emotion of his speech so that his hatful of assorted artillery rattled gently.

Sheriff Casper handed the weapon back to Prudence with the cartridges separate. "I wouldn't put them shells back in there if I was you, ma'am. If that old gun went off, it'd likely blow out the side of a house."

The Sheriff and his deputy turned and started back up the aisle. When they reached the front of the bus, Sheriff Casper picked up the driver's microphone and addressed the passengers. "Well, folks, my deputy here will return yer personal property now, and that's about all and we want to apologize for holdin' you up this way and we're glad to be able to cause you no further trouble, everybody bein' properly identified as bein' innocent citizens. Happy trip, folks."

Deputy Williams arrived at the front of the bus, having returned all the weapons to their owners, and the two sheriffs left.

Marshall wiped the sweat from his forehead and said under his breath, "Son of a bitch, those two nutty old bags."

Julian eyed him and said, "W-w-what happened?"

Marshall turned upon him irritably, "Didn't I tell you to cut out the goddamn stammer?"

"Uh huh."

"Well, then say it right."

Julian did. "What happened?" Then he added, "Are you scared again?"

Marshall said, "No, I'm not and stop asking that. When I am, I'll let you know. But, it wouldn't have been funny if those cops had been after us, would it?"

"But, what were they . . . ?" And then, as an afterthought, "Why did you tell them my name was Herman?"

Marshall wondered what it would be like if he really had a kid brother like Julian. Were all kids like that? He supposed so. He probably had been himself. His sense of humor reasserted itself and he replied, "I once had a parrot by that name. He could talk your head off. What happened was that those two biddies thought we were hijackers and told the driver."

Julian said, "Hijackers! Say, gee, that would be fun." He whipped his Bubble Gun from its holster and pressed it against Marshall's side. "I ain't aimin' to hurt anybody long as you stay nice and quiet in your seat, but I wouldn't like this thing to go off because it sure makes a powerful hole. Driver, turn around, we ain't goin' to Washington. We're goin' to . . . What was the name of that place in Mexico?"

The Coote sisters, anxious to mollify the pair opposite for their error, had been gazing over and listening.

Prudence said, "Oh, isn't he sweet!" and gave her most winning smile.

Marshall threw a poisonous look in return, muttered, "Oh, for chrissakes," pulled his ten-gallon hat down over his eyes and slumped low in his seat again. Unaccountably, and from far out in left field, he suddenly found himself wondering how the chess game on Bus 396 was getting on. Beneath him the tires droned their way to Washington.

In a secret engineering laboratory somewhere in Moscow a burly Russian engineer high up in the Party hierarchy achieved the completion of the object on which he was working alone and under heavy guard. It took five passes and passwords to get through five locked doors to reach him. Himself a rocket designer and arms expert, on this he had worked alone, since not even technicians were allowed in to handle the lathes, welding equipment and precision tools.

The technician hefted the finished object in his hand, sighed and laid it down on the workbench before him. A red light flashed onto a panel high up on the wall opposite, which meant that someone from the outside had begun the long routine of penetrating the laboratory. It would be someone properly identified. Nevertheless, the man, as a precaution, threw a cloth over the object and waited. It took fifteen minutes for the visitor to pass all the challenges and enter. He wore the insignia of an Army colonel on the epaulettes of his gray greatcoat and the peak of his cap, but the engineer recognized him as a character of dual pursuits, holding even higher rank in the branch of Soviet counterespionage.

The expert said, "Comrade Veznin."

The officer said, "Comrade Vosnevsky," and then added, "Have you completed it?"

"Yes."

He removed the cloth from the object.

The Colonel picked it up, opened and examined it. Then he gave Vosnevsky a long, hard stare. The latter, who was valuable enough and sufficiently high in the Party not to care, returned the look.

12

They had passed the Continental
Divide, but the snowy peaks of the
Sangre de Cristo Range were visible
behind them in the distance, and
Marshall explained it to Julian as a kind
of knife edge sharply dividing rainfall so
that the drops falling on one side would
run off eastwards while those dropping
a few inches away would head west and
wind up in the Pacific Ocean or the
Gulf of California.

At least that was the way Marshall
saw it graphically and explained it to
Julian, who took it as gospel and
thought of himself as being perched
upon the topmost spine of the ridge in
the wintertime with a sled, trying to
make up his mind whether he would
slide down to the east or to the west.

Marshall illuminated the boredom of the endless plains and wheatfields of Kansas with the saga of "Bleeding Kansas," remembered from his high school history days when, himself a Westerner, born in Abilene, he had understood something of the bloody convulsions that had shaken that state. Through his eyes Julian saw Northerners, Southerners, soldiers, rebels, pioneers in covered wagons, outlaws and gunslingers.

Marshall never talked down to Julian or lectured or attempted to impress him, probably because actually he was talking more to himself than the boy and trying to revive some of his own lost faith.

He had gone from high school into the Army in a mood half of adventurous recklessness, half from conviction, to train to become both an accomplished killer as well as an avoider of death. He had served his tour in Vietnam to return to a headless, mindless, embittered country, a large part of whose people had looked upon him as a fool and a sucker to the point where he had stripped his insignia from his jacket and kept his mouth shut about his service. But the defeatism of his country and his countrymen and their almost total cynicism had infected him. He had returned with a stake of some three thousand dollars in pay as well as a tribute to his skill as a crapshooter and had crisscrossed a number of states looking not so much for work as for any road to quick and easy money that was not criminal. The University dream was gone. The G.I. Bill or anything to do with the Army filled him with disgust. It was too late. Somewhere there must be a main chance and as he roved and searched his capital dwindled away. He had taken jobs here and there but none of them offered any future.

Then someone had said Washington was the place. If you got to know the right people, the pickings could be astronomical. He didn't quite believe this but it did seem that a guy who knew his way around a bit could do himself some good. Hence, his destination.

They crossed the Mississippi at its confluence with the Missouri at St. Louis. Marshall made it an event for Julian as well as for himself for he was remembering his Mark Twain as he looked upon the broad, yellow, sluggish, swirling waters, and he had once made a short trip on that river in an old stern-wheeler and so could picture for Julian the days of the river gamblers and double-barreled derringers fired under tables when an ace too many made its appearance.

To Julian, the hours, the days and the nights of rolling across the country were as close to heaven as any small boy had the right to expect. He had earned the friendship, respect and companionship of an adult who treated him like a man. He had lived through the maddest kind of storybook adventure in which he had played a real-life part as a hero, though curiously that incident left less impression upon his memory than the joys of the trip and the equality of his footing with Marshall.

For they lived during that time as men on the loose and far away from the supervision of women or anyone else. They washed when they were able and it was convenient, or didn't, and abused their stomachs at all hours of the morning, noon or night with dubious frankfurters, doubtful hamburgers as well as other kinds of burgers, greasy french fries, stale sandwiches, candy bars, ice cream cones, all washed down with every variety of cola, orange, grapefruit or cherry drink, milk, tea and coffee. Even in that short time Julian blossomed and filled out. It was sheer bliss.

And yet, for Marshall, all the time what he knew he would do when the opportunity presented itself was at the back of his mind, he hating it, despising himself and yet uncontrollably certain. He wasn't even sure whether it had anything to do with his attitude towards the boy and the trouble he took with him. Julian appealed to him, had even touched him, because he was a "nothing" child with a one-track mind and a dreamer with the courage to attempt to grasp the dream.

"Nothing" to Marshall's way of thinking was complimentary and not derogatory, for Julian had very few of the irritating traits of the small boy. He wasn't a smart aleck or a know-it-all, he wasn't fresh or too prying and could take no or shut up for an answer. His obvious coddling by his mother and, if it was true, neglect by his father had endowed him with an appealing innocence that led him to accept what came simply as a part of things, either as they were or as they seemed to be, and whatever gap there was between the two he filled in with his fantasy. And besides which there was the worship he bestowed upon Marshall with every look and gesture and the complete faith as evinced by the instantaneous cure of his stammer.

This worship, this love—Marshall's corrupt mind fled from these words as though they themselves were corruption. They were extremely painful for him to contemplate, painful to the point where they could not be entertained and had to be pushed back and altered to the state where they were no longer connected with what he intended to do. His plan had now simply become an automatism waiting upon the moment, and his impatience was growing, as two thirds of the distance across the continent had been covered.

Oddly enough, while the plan had germinated far, far back, Marshall could hardly remember the day or the time that Julian had returned to his seat clutching his diagram and reporting that the Colonel had said it would work, after which, of course, there had been the graphic demonstration. It had been the episode of the silly Coote sisters that had crystallized the necessity for early action.

It was while he was being frisked by the Sheriff that he realized the danger not only to his own safety and freedom in connection with this crazy caper, but also of the immediate jeopardy of losing his chance for the big stake. But for the thickheadedness of the Sheriff and his deputy and the fact that they had been alerted to look for an armed hijacker and not a fugitive boy, it could have been disastrous.

And so when at last the opportunity did present itself the automatism which had lain dormant at the back of Marshall's mind took over. One moment he had been glancing down at Julian with an expression of mingled affection and compassion as he wondered what his father was really like and how much of a fool the man could be, and the next his look was one of all the cunning that had been superimposed upon his nature.

It was 1:30 in the morning and they were approaching Pittsburgh. A difference in the music of the tires caused by a change in the roadbed awakened Marshall and through the window he could see the glow of Pittsburgh's furnaces daubing the ceiling of the night sky with pale orange. That was when Marshall looked upon Julian curled up with his head on his Buffalo Bill jacket sound asleep in the seat next to him. It had induced his sympathy and affection until he saw an edge of the diagram of the Bubble Gun showing from the pocket of Julian's coat, far enough from the sleeping boy's head for the chance to remove it.

The bus driver's voice boomed loudly over the loud-speaker, "Coming into Pittsburgh, folks. Forty-five minutes' break for refreshments if you want any or a wash-up, but keep an eye on the time and don't miss the bus. Departure two thirty-five A.M."

All through the noisy announcement which brought the other passengers astir Marshall kept his eye on Julian but the boy never moved. He threw a glance across to the only two who might have observed his actions, but the Coote sisters were already moving down the aisle. They always disembarked no matter where or how brief the stop. Then, with infinite care and patience so that there was not so much as a whisper of a rustle from the sheet of paper, Marshall drew the diagram of the Bubble Gun from Julian's pocket and put it in his own. Pittsburgh was a major metropolis. What he needed would surely be available there at the terminal.

But first he had to slip out of his seat without waking Julian. He had hung back to let all the others disembark first and to see whether the effect of their bustle as well as the traffic sounds and the night noises from without would disturb Julian. But the boy had only shifted his position slightly and thereafter was dead to the world.

The coin-operated photocopier was situated next to a

stamp vending machine which at that time of the morning was not being greatly patronized. Marshall watched
the area and for a good ten minutes no one touched
either of the machines. The Coote sisters were not in
sight. He thought they were probably accepting the bus
driver's invitation to wash up, nor did he see any of the
other passengers from their bus. Even at that early hour
there was much movement through the terminal. Marshall went over to the copying machine. He knew exactly
what he had to do and how to do it.

Taking the diagram of the Bubble Gun from his
pocket, he flattened it out, then producing an envelope
he carefully tore a white square from the back and wrote
upon it. He placed this on the diagram and drew a heavy
border on the square, saw that it was properly positioned, slid the diagram into the slot, inserted his quarter
and waited the few seconds it took the machine to hiss
and grumble, perform its function and deliver him his
photocopy. He plucked it forth and examined it with
satisfaction and invested two more coins for additional
copies. He then retrieved the original diagram and
removed the piece of envelope back, which he shredded
into tiny bits and dropped into a refuse basket. He pock-
eted Julian's drawing and once more carefully examined
the photocopy. Where in the lower-right-hand corner it
had once read, THE BUBBLE GUN, INVENTED BY JULIAN
WEST, 137 EAST VIEW TERRACE, SAN DIEGO, CALIFORNIA,
APRIL 25, 1973, it now read, TOY BUBBLE GUN, INVENTED
BY FRANK MARSHALL, 39 ORCHARD ST., ABILENE, TEXAS,
APRIL 3, 1973. The border he had drawn about this leg-
end had blended perfectly and completely concealed the

fact that a new address and inventor had been superimposed.

Just for luck, in case someone passing by might have
recognized him, Marshall moved over to the stamp machine and played it for a couple of quarters, and what he
thought of when the stamps began to issue was a jackpot
and a never ending cascade of money tumbling from a
one-armed bandit.

From then on Marshall found himself involved in the
most dangerous moments. The photocopies stowed
away in an inside pocket, and that much successfully
accomplished without being seen, he could move freely
about the waiting room. But what if Julian woke in the
meantime? How to get the paper back into his pocket
again unobserved? Go back now, or wait for general
boarding?

You learned under fire to figure the odds, play them
and stick to them. The sooner he got back to the bus
before the passengers began piling on, the better. He
would, or he wouldn't, find Julian awake and sitting up
perhaps, not yet aware that his diagram had been ab-
stracted, but the odds read that with all still quiet in the
bus he ought not to have awakened. But to Marshall's
surprise, he found that now that he had done it and there
was no longer that automatism to regulate his conduct
he was badly shaken, nervous and frightened.

Marshall went to the all-night bar and bought himself
a double Jack Daniels, as insurance in case he had to face
the kid, knocked it back and walked to the bus. He felt
that the noises all about, the motors, the departures and
arrivals and loudspeaker announcements were shatter-

ing. He was sweating and quite ridiculously found himself walking on tiptoes to his seat to find Julian was still fast asleep and almost in the same position. The Coote sisters had not yet returned, the bus was half empty. It was no problem at all, carefully and delicately to restore Julian's diagram to his pocket exactly as it had been before. This done, he settled himself back into his half-dozing position and was actually asleep when, with the full complement of passengers for Washington, they pulled away from the terminal.

13

The shaft of the Washington Monument in the distance poked its pencil point into the low-heat haze of the hot, sticky morning air heavily freighted with the fumes of vehicular traffic. Marshall and Julian stood transfixed by a feeling of sudden strangeness and mutual embarrassment which had descended like a curtain to separate the boy and the man, cut them off from the camaraderie that had characterized their relationship during the trip, and they remained there on the sidewalk almost as strangers once again. A line of cabs was drawn up at the curb.

It had been close to ten o'clock in the morning when they had emerged from the bus, each with his one piece of hand luggage, and marched unhindered through the humming Washington, D.C., bus station.

By bringing attention to themselves with their bizarre costumes they, by some reverse principle, attracted no attention beyond the momentary glance of one policeman on duty in the terminal as well as that of one or two passersby.

Marshall next had changed into his old, stripped-down battle jacket again, carried his Western hat instead of wearing it, and the fact that he had a small boy in a Buffalo Bill outfit in tow attracted no more notice than did the frantic mother of a recalcitrant six year old clad in a space suit, whose face from time to time she attempted to slap through his helmet. Thus Marshall and Julian passed unchallenged into the city of their destination. The large clock outside the terminal showed the time as 10:13 and even as they watched it clicked over to 10:14.

The solidness of their being there, the feeling of the hot cement pavement beneath their feet, the overwhelming presence of the Capital City testifying to the end of their journey, had thrown Marshall into a state bordering on confusion, the confusion mixed with guilt and worry, plus the sense of the passage of time as the horrid clock now showed 10:15 and he realized he had no fixed plan.

With Julian it was more a matter of the innate tact which some children possess or perhaps more the fear of offending a grownup. He had set out for Washington and now in Washington he was. But he was very well aware that without Marshall things might have been very different. He had been helped over dangers, some half realized or only guessed at, and there was no doubt but that for Marshall and the truck ride to Albuquerque he would probably at that moment be back home in San Diego. And then there had been the matter of the little affair of the hand grenade which none of the press had got straight as to exactly what had happened. But Julian knew. Dead is a difficult thing for man wholly to imagine even when in battle he is threatened with immediate extinction, for a child almost impossible. Yet Julian remembered the roar and the volcano of dirt, smoke, metal, stones and cabbage leaves that had erupted in the neighboring field.

Well, but now here was private business with no more than a taxi ride separating him from the Patent Office and the final realization of his dream. He did not know how either to say goodbye or to show his gratitude, nor at that moment, as again the clock fired another minute backwards into eternity, did Marshall.

It was Julian who gave Marshall the opening he needed in some way to prepare Julian, even slightly, for what might be going to happen and what he was about to do to him.

The boy had set his suitcase down and was still clutching the toy rifle. He now fingered his flowing moustache and goatee and asked, "Should I still keep these on?"

The question yanked Marshall's scattered thoughts back onto the more orderly track of question and answer and he replied, "What? Oh, yeah, sure, kid, you better. It got us past those cops, didn't it?"

Marshall had been certain that all terminals would be watched but the scrutiny upon their arrival had been purely perfunctory since once again the official obtuseness of not looking for a runaway boy from San Diego to arrive on a bus from L.A. could be counted upon. Besides which there was Buffalo Bill, and Marshall felt the longer Julian was able to keep to this disguise, the better. What Marshall didn't want for at least twenty-four hours, or at the very least twelve, was a hullabaloo over Julian West, his discovery and his invention and so he repeated, "Yeah, yeah, kid, sure. You look okay. Nobody will recognize you."

Julian now essayed a tentative trial at parting. He said, "Well . . . gee . . . thanks for everything . . . you were great."

Marshall said, "That's alright. You're not so bad yourself."

Julian said, "You know, I mean, you were really great . . . If you hadn't thrown away the bomb . . . I mean the grenade, we . . ."

Marshall said, "That's okay. If you hadn't distracted that loony son of a bitch when you did I could be lying up in a mortuary parlor in El Paso with a bullet through my skull waiting for someone to come and collect me."

Julian's mind did an instant replay of the scene and he asked, "Would he really have shot you?"

Marshall replied, "Yes, he would."

Julian had a new thought. He said, "Then you were just pretending to be scared so that maybe . . ."

Marshall said, "No, I wasn't. I was scared for real. Good and."

Julian looked up at him and pulled at his lower lip.

Marshall said, "Look, kid, there isn't time to go into

this now but after you've been around a while you learn
that there are times to be scared and others not to be.
But you can't always pick 'em. See?"

Julian was gravely and curiously satisfied. Since he had
left home there seemed to be a number of things now
that he could see or somewhat understand that he never
could before.

People by ones, twos or threes got into cabs waiting
end to end, slammed the door shut with a violent thunk
and gave instructions to the driver. The front cabs drove
away, the next cabs moved up.

Marshall had one more try. He said, "Look here,
Julian, do you know anything at all about how the Patent
Office operates?"

The question and the expression on Marshall's face
was concomitant with Julian's own nervousness and he
reached for the diagram. "Well, I go and show them this
and the . . ." and here he patted the Bubble Gun in its
absurd Western holster.

Marshall said, "Listen, maybe you ought to know. It
isn't all that simple. See, they've got to make a search and
maybe somebody else thought of it first."

Julian refused even to consider this and said, "Aw, I'll
bet nobody ever thought of this before."

But Marshall was insistent on somehow trying to condition the boy for the catastrophe he was preparing for
him.

He said, "Well, maybe even something like it, you
know. See, a lot of people get ideas which are almost the
same."

Julian said, "That's why I better hurry. I gotta get mine

in first, don't I?" And his gaze into Marshall's face was so straightforwardly innocent that the deviousness of Marshall's own mind at that moment forced him to wonder whether Julian was masking and actually suspected him of what he was up to and about to do, but the moment passed and he realized there was no guile in the purely practical statement.

He said, "Look, Julian, you do know what you're doing, don't you?"

Julian nodded and said, "Uh huh," and wondered why Marshall was going on like this.

"You haven't got a grandmother here, have you?"

Julian shook his head and said, "No. She lives in Olympia, but that's Washington too, isn't it? So it wasn't really a lie."

"Where are you gonna stay tonight?"

Julian shrugged and replied, "Somewhere. I've got some money left."

Marshall had one more try. "Oughtn't we maybe to phone your old man?"

Julian shook his head emphatically. "He wouldn't care. He's too busy. Mom would start screaming." Then he added, "I've got to go to the Patent Office."

Marshall's good impulses faded. He, too, had to get to the Patent Office and what was more, with a head start. And he'd got to stop worrying about Julian. If anything was a sure thing it was that sooner or later the cops would pick him up and send him home. He would come to no harm.

Marshall said, "Okay, we'll get a cab and I'll drop you off there." Then, without further ado, he began the perpetration of his black deed. "Hey, wait a minute, I forgot. I gotta make a phone call. I'll be back in a sec."

He turned and was off, leaving Julian standing on the sidewalk, uncertain as to whether he was further upset by the delay or pleased that the total separation from Marshall was not yet to be.

Marshall wasted no further time. He reentered the bus station, hurried through the waiting room and exited the other side, where an arriving cab discharged a fare. He held the door open while a man and woman got out and paid.

Marshall then asked, "Okay?"

"Uh huh. Where to?"

Marshall said, "The Patent Office," got in, shut the door and was driven off.

It took some twenty minutes of standing, a solitary and slightly absurd figure, outside the bus station, before Julian realized that something had perhaps gone amiss, though adults often did chatter for ages on the telephone. Maybe Marshall was talking to his girl. The suspicion that he had been ditched never at any time entered his mind. He decided to wait another five minutes and then go and look. Now, further uncertain, he gave it ten and then went back into the bus station where he found the banks of public telephone booths, but none of them contained anyone even resembling Marshall and he then fell prey to the sudden panic that he might have missed him in the crowd or that Marshall had now returned to their rendezvous, so he ran to the door and looked out at where he had been standing, but there was no sign of his friend. He wandered back into the terminal hoping to catch a glimpse of him. Marshall had said he would be right back and in so doing had put a requirement upon Julian to wait for him.

But even as he threaded through the passing throng, continuing his search, Julian suddenly became aware that he was attracting attention and was being noticed by people turning to look at him. Intuition, plus some of the hard practical wisdom of Marshall that had rubbed off on him during the voyage, caught him up. As long as he had been in the company of his "big brother," Marshall, no one had paid any attention, but now by himself, unaccompanied, in this outfit he was highly conspicuous.

Julian drifted out of the maelstrom of passenger traffic to the shops and rest rooms at the side, and in one section, half concealed, he came upon a corner where the cleaners kept their gear. There was no one there and Julian quickly stripped off his moustache and goatee and then divested himself of the Buffalo Bill outfit which he stuffed into his suitcase, resuming his leather jacket and putting on his glasses again. The toy rifle was too long to fit into his bag which had managed to take the cartridge belt and holster. The Bubble Gun he restored once more to his right-hand jacket pocket. Then, closing the suitcase, he stood the rifle up in a corner with the mops and brooms, gave it a last regretful look, turned away and emerged from the cleaners' nook exactly the same small boy who boarded Bus 396 in San Diego, California, so many ages ago.

Well, not exactly the same boy. He found himself missing Marshall. He missed him dreadfully, to the point where he was close to being frightened.

If there had never been a Marshall it would have been different. He would have wandered through his dream-world untouched, unimpinged upon, following along the line of least resistance but always moving towards his objective guided by the pot of gold at the end of the rainbow. But there had been Marshall, tall, handsome, laughing with those funny eyes that could light up almost as though there was a battery behind them. There had been the Marshall—the touch of whose firm hand had been more of a comfort than the man had realized—the Marshall who had fed him, looked after him, talked to him, treated him like a man and seemed to take him seriously. Now he was gone, vanished into the crowd or from the face of the earth as though he had never existed. He had left no address, nothing but a memory, and Julian realized a void such as he had never felt before. He wished now that he had not changed from Buffalo Bill, almost as though in divesting himself of those marvelous garments which had played such a part in their adventurous escape he had also somehow divested himself of Marshall. He was no nearer the answer to his friend's disappearance. It had to be accepted as one of those things that happened. Kids got lost and yelled for their mothers. Why shouldn't grownups, too, get lost? He thought for a moment of going to the information desk and asking to have Marshall called for over the loud-speakers and then said to himself, "Boy, would that be a great idea! Tell everybody where we are."

He picked up his case. It wouldn't do to linger in that terminal with the police on the lookout. When he had left home filled with his determination to patent his invention and show his father, there had been no Marshall. So there was no Marshall now and he was just one cab ride away from the end of the line. He pulled himself together, picked up his little case and strode purposefully through the waiting room to the exit.

Julian went to the head of the cab line where the driver, a black, was lounging, reading the morning paper, and asked, "Are you free?"

The driver, who was youngish, pleasant-looking and with a quirk to his lips as though most things that he encountered amused him, looked up from his newspaper and into the face of the small boy which appeared at his window level and gave him a kind of shock, as though he had seen him somewhere before and ought to be saying, "Why, hello there," instead of, as he did, "Uh? Yes, sure. Where do you want to go, sonny?"

Julian replied, "The Patent Office, please. The place where they patent inventions."

The driver put aside his reading and shifted his body to a more alert position. "The Patent Office?" he repeated. "Now, what do you think you're going to do there?" You could never tell with kids. Sometimes they just string you along for the hell of it.

Julian replied, "Patent my invention."

Now slightly startled, the man repeated, "Patent your invention? Well, what do you know! Starting early, aren't you? That's about a three-dollar trip across the river. Don't get me wrong, kid, but I'm running a business. Have you got any money?"

"Oh, that's alright," Julian said, reached into his pocket and produced what he had left, some thirty-three dollars and small change.

The driver glanced at it, his eyes bulging. Then he smiled and said exaggeratedly, "Excuse *me*," and then added, "SIR," in capital letters. "Get in. You got yourself a ride."

Julian said, "Okay. Thanks," and got in asking, "Do you want it now or later?"

"Later will be just fine," the driver said as he moved off.

Julian sat back and studied the license card of the driver framed behind cellophane and mounted in the cab. It showed a photograph of him and said that his name was Meech Morrow, age thirty-eight, M for married and a number.

The sliding window between them was open and Julian asked, "Is it far, Mr. Morrow?"

The driver replied, "About ten minutes," and then gave vent to a chuckle. "Mr. Morrow! That's a good one. What's your name?"

Julian had been on the verge of blurting it out but remembered that this might be unwise and then was suddenly tickled by another memory which made him want to giggle and replied, "Herman."

"Well, Mr. Herman," Morrow said, "we'll have you there in a jiffy. Just you sit back in the seat comfortable like it says on the sign."

Julian looked and indeed found there was a warning posted advising, "Passengers will please oblige by sitting well back in case of sudden stops."

Julian nestled himself well into a corner, took a grip upon a strap that seemed to be hanging there conveniently and gave himself up to a refresher course in the golden dream when every child in every block would be wanting a Bubble Gun invented and patented by Julian West.

As Meech Morrow's cab edged its way through downtown Washington's mid-morning traffic in the direction of the Potomac Bridge, other events that were to affect the life and times of that same Julian West, inventor, were taking place.

At Crystal City, Virginia, just across the river from Washington, Frank Marshall emerged from the building of the United States Department of Commerce where the Patent Office was located, with a number of forms, booklets and papers in his hand and an expression of brisk satisfaction and a current of energy and decision on his face. He glanced at his wristwatch, which registered eleven o'clock, then looked about him a moment to orient himself. He consulted an address upon a sheet of paper, walked quickly to a neighboring office building where he studied the lobby directory, which was three-quarters filled with the names of patent attorneys. The rest of the directory board was devoted to engineering, drafting and research firms concerned with assisting would-be inventors in meeting all the requirements of the Patent Office. Marshall noted down the name of one such drafting firm which seemed to occupy an entire floor of the building, chose that of a patent attorney and then headed for the bank of elevators. With any luck and the investment of the last of his cash resources, he might still be able to file at the Patent Office before closing time.

Buried in the vast complex of the Pentagon Building, the photograph of Richard Milhous Nixon, captured in a moment of Presidential nobility, was looking down from the wall of the conference room where Major-General Thomas H. Horgan was presiding over a meeting numbering two generals, three colonels, several CIA men and a pair from the FBI. Horgan was engaged in chewing out Colonel John Sisson, and at that moment was saying, "Jesus Christ, John, you sure screwed this one up. What the hell was it that son of a bitch photographed anyway?"

Sisson was a man not easily cowed, but it was the absurdity of it all rather than the battery of angry looks fired at him from all around the long table that was throwing him, and he replied inanely, "Well, er—I—er —I guess it was a Bubble Gun."

Horgan's voice rose, "What? Bubblegum? What the hell are you talking about? For chrissakes, speak clearly!"

Sisson stammered, "I didn't say b-b-bubblegum," and suddenly found himself ridiculously wafted back to the bus and the little boy who also stammered sitting by his side. "I said a Bubble Gun. A pistol that shot bubbles."

Horgan's voice went up another decibel, "That shot what? Oh, my God, what the hell did it look like? You said there was a diagram? Well, what kind of a diagram?"

Sisson tried to think back to what it had looked like, but if his life had depended upon it he could not have reproduced it at that moment and he had to blurt out, "Well, sir, I never really paid too much attention to it. There was something about a washer in the wrong place. You know, it was just a kid bothering me and then before I knew it . . ."

General Horgan completed the sentence for him.

". . . the stupid bastard photographed it, and made the American Army look like a pack of goddamn fools."

A general with one star less, but from a different department, now sought to come to the rescue of the unhappy Sisson. He said to Horgan, "Now wait a minute, Tom, maybe it isn't so bad. Okay, the Russians put a set of phony rocket plans in our hands. You were smart enough to spot them. We organize a set of phony plans of our own to show them we want them to cut out the kidding so we can both stop wasting our time on a lot of crap. So, what's the difference as long as they get the message?"

Horgan refused to be mollified, and still furious, snarled, "The difference is a goddamn foul-up and we don't know where the hell we're at. Besides which, we've been saving up that Russian pigeon, Allon, for years until we wanted to use him and now we've got him to blow his cover for nothing." He pointed his finger at Sisson. "Listen, I don't give a goddamn how you do it or where you get it from, but I want to see that diagram before tomorrow. I want to know just what the hell they've got."

The other general who had spoken up asked, "What became of the kid, John?"

Sisson replied miserably, "I don't know. He just disappeared. Haven't you been reading the papers?" He felt put upon and needed a scapegoat, and turned to the FBI men. "Listen, can't you guys find a boy whose description has been broadcast all over the country? And I thought you were supposed to stop that thing from leaving the country."

One of the FBI men said, "The hell we were. That was

a CIA job. And the child isn't a kidnapping case. That's for the local fuzz."

One of the CIA men retorted angrily, "Listen, lay off us. I suppose you trigger-happy bastards would have shot up that Mexican airport. For chrissakes."

The second general said, "Oh, cut it out. It's one of those things. Look, let's go back and get the whole thing from the beginning again and maybe we can see some daylight. John, you say you had Allon nicely hooked and set up, but when was it exactly this kid braced you? He wouldn't have been in cahoots with Allon, would he?"

"Oh for godsakes, no. A ten year old?" Sisson continued: "All I can tell you is that . . ." And here again he launched into his story, racking his brain to try to remember every scrap that might bear upon the subject or give a clue. The men around the table listened silently. A glance of one of the CIA men drifted to the portrait photograph of the President and a stab of light upon the sheet of glass over it gave him the impression momentarily of an eyebrow having gone up.

The steel and glass mountain of the United States Department of Commerce Building completed the obliteration of the world of fantasy in which Julian had been voyaging and jolted him into the terror of reality.

ANYONE CAN PATENT AN INVENTION had been the smooth, seductive headline in his *Popular Mechanics* magazine, which had seduced him into that first step in attaining that goal.

But he wasn't "anyone," that anonymous genius whose rights to the protection of his invention were defined and protected by law. He was Julian West, age nine and a half, fifth grade, Elias P. Johnson Preparatory School, San Diego, California, with a messy, worked-over diagram in one pocket and a slightly dubiously performing Bubble Gun in the other. San Diego was a million miles away and here was Washington to which somehow he had got himself transported, and behind these sets of revolving doors which were kept in a constant twirl by people pushing in and out was—well, was whatever it was that happened to an invention that enabled one to call it "patented."

Julian got out of the cab and stood on the sidewalk facing the building, for a moment thrust back once more into the world of giants and giantism. Children, in the make-believe in which most of them live, adjust themselves to an outsized world, but every so often they find themselves a race of Lilliputians dwarfed by a planet peopled with Brobdingnagians more overwhelming and terrifying than ever imagined by Swift. Everything looms over the child. His parents, his teachers, chairs, tables, lamps. Until he meets with his playmates his looks are always upwards. Everything peers down at him. If he could not see himself equipped with Excalibur or a Ray-gun, how could he survive in a world of perpetual optical menace? The bus ride from beginning to end had been a fairy tale. How was anyone to understand the feelings of a small boy faced with his first real plunge into the terrors of an uncaring adult world far removed from every shelter and every security he had ever known?

But in a curious way Meech Morrow did, not so much because of the fact that he had children of his own but rather because of the figure that Julian cut. Looking at the back of the boy not quite four feet tall from the soles of his Keds to the top of his carroty hair, paper suitcase in his hand, one sock up and one sock down, the head tilted just slightly backwards as though not wishing or even daring to look as high as to the top of the building, Morrow's heart was penetrated by the absurdity of his project and his fearful loneliness. Whether the whole thing was a make-up or the child actually believed he had created something which was patentable, the pathos of the moment was almost unbearable. Besides which there was something nibbling at the back of Morrow's mind, from the first moment of shock when he had wanted to say hello as though to someone he had recognized. Where had he seen him before? Whatever, Morrow knew that to abandon him was unthinkable and so he said, "I'll wait for you."

Julian, startled, turned and plunged his hand into his pocket. He said, "Aw gee, I forgot for a minute but I wasn't going to go away without paying you, honest."

Morrow said, "I know you weren't, sonny, but I better stay. You can pay me when you come out. Maybe you'll be needing another ride somewhere. I'll stop the clock."

Julian said, "Aw, you got work to do," but some of the fear had been drained out of him. He was no longer completely alone. Somebody was standing by.

Morrow laughed and said, "That's alright, kid. Maybe I'm just curious what goes on inside there. Nobody ever told me. You go ahead and tell 'em about your invention and I'll be here when you come out."

Comfort and courage flowed back into Julian again as

he thought to himself, *Frank Marshall would have done that, too.* He said, "Okay, thanks. It shouldn't take long. I'll hurry up." And he marched steadfastly across the intervening pavement and was whirled within by the revolving door.

Meech Morrow watched him go and then turned to the well at the side of the driver's seat where he kept his city maps, log book, reading matter, old newspapers and scrabbled until he found what he was looking for, a two-day-old newspaper. He opened it to page three, read the story there once again, looked at the photograph and began a chuckle that grew into a laugh. "Well, goddamn," he said to himself. "Ain't that something: Mr. Herman," and repeated, "Well goddamn," and then added, "Ain't that some kid."

In the office of Peabody and Wilson, Drafting Engineers and Patent Consultants, a young man, using a reversed pen as a pointer, was smiling at a photocopy of a diagram laid on the table before him.

He said, "That's amusing. How come you thought of that?"

Frank Marshall said, "My kid brother had a water pistol. He gave it to me to fix when it busted and when I took it apart I thought maybe, you know, like bubbles through those rings."

The draftsman nodded and said, "Uh huh," and then pointing with his pen, said, "Which line here? The heavy or the light one?"

Marshall said quickly, "The light one, where I corrected it in pencil. See, this bag was too close to the nozzle and . . ."

"Yeah, sure. Have you got a model?"

For the first time, Marshall felt an anxiety. Could he have got the gun away from Julian too?

He asked, "Do I have to have one?"

"Not really. They'd prefer it if you had, but your diagram is clear and you could put the model in later."

Marshall asked, "How long will it take? I'm in a hurry."

The draftsman smiled and said, "They always are," and then, chewing the end of the pen, "Not too long. The Patent Office closes at five. We could do it by four. In the meantime you could be filling out all the rest of the forms. By the way, you know the filing fee is sixty-five bucks?"

Marshall said, "Uh huh. And what about your drawing?"

"Half a C."

Marshall nodded and said, "That's okay," and thought of the hole this would make in his remaining capital. But if he got his patent . . . He asked, "You couldn't make it by 3:30, could you?"

The draftsman said, "I'll try." They were always in a hurry, these inventors, even with the craziest ideas, always terrified that someone might get in ahead of them.

14

It was after a wait of some twenty
minutes that Morrow saw Julian
emerge, or rather erupt from the
revolving door as someone in haste
behind him practically catapulted him
out. He saw that the boy was clutching
pamphlets, folders and forms and as he
recovered himself and slowly
approached the cab Morrow said,
"Well, Mr. Julian, how did you make
out?" and was immediately sorry that
he had done so, that is to say, called
him by his right name, for to the
already dazed expression on Julian's
face now was added terror.

For an instant he thought the boy
was going to turn and run, and Julian,
his false identity so easily pierced, for a

moment had actually been minded to do so. Then he remembered that he had not paid the cab man and remained on the pavement, a picture of abject misery and fright, clutching his sheaves of bumph.

Meech Morrow reached over and opened the front door of the cab on the other side from the driver's seat. He said, "You just come and sit here alongside me and we'll have a little chat. You got nothing to be afraid of with Meech Morrow."

Julian got in and Morrow closed the door. The driver said, "You're the boy I read about in the paper, but we'll forget about that. Did you sure enough have an invention? What happened in there? They give you the run-around?"

Julian shook his head slowly and said, "No, I guess not. They were busy. A man asked if I'd researched it and if I hadn't I ought to." He was looking up at Morrow but his eyes were turned inwards to the bureaucratic turmoil through which he had been whirled with the short shrift that a small boy with a much folded and dirtied diagram might expect.

Passing through those revolving doors he had gone from fantasy to a nightmare of instructions, "Go there," "Do this," "Room 428," "Second door on the left," "Can't talk to you now, sonny, I'm too busy," "Here, take this home, read it and come back with your father."

Julian tried to tell some of it to Morrow. He said, "It's gotta be on some kind of special paper with special kinds of instruments and I have to take it to a patent attorney. What's a patent attorney?"

Morrow said with a faint note of contempt in his voice,

one people often have when speaking of the legal profession, "Lawyers. I guess maybe there's a lot of legal stuff about getting a patent."

Julian was shifting the pamphlets unhappily on his lap and remembering. He said, "Indian ink only. Why does it have to be with ink made by Indians?"

Morrow said, "Not Indian. India. I guess maybe it doesn't smudge or rub out."

Julian said, "A man told me that all drawings had to be made with drafting instruments."

Morrow reached over and took one of the pamphlets and thumbed through it and said, "Oh boy. 'Written document of petition,' 'Oath of declaration,' 'Drawing on pure white paper of the thickness corresponding to two- or three-ply Bristol board.' Brother, they don't make it easy."

A man stuck his head inside the cab window and asked, "This cab free?"

Morrow replied respectfully, "No sir, I'm afraid not," flipped on his ignition and drove off a way before stopping and saying to Julian, "Maybe you better get in the back seat and then nobody will ask me."

Julian did as he was told and once in the back of the cab relapsed into that helpless feeling of nightmare from which he was trying to wake up and could not.

Morrow looked back and said, "Okay, what do we do now?"

As Morrow watched, Julian drew his diagram from his pocket and unfolded it. He regarded it for a moment and then said, "I haven't got any special kind of paper." Something had fluttered to the floor, a piece of white pasteboard. Julian picked it up and Morrow was surprised at the sudden change of expression that came over the boy's face. Julian handed him the card and said, "Could we go there?"

Morrow looked at the name and address and whistled with astonishment. He asked, "You know him, boy?"

Julian nodded. "He helped me with what was wrong with my invention. I mean, on the bus. He said if I got into any kind of trouble . . ."

Morrow said, "Kid, I'd say you sure got some muscle there. Want to go see him?"

"Yes, please."

Morrow said, "No charge for the waiting time. Like I said, it's strictly business. That's a four-dollar trip. Okay?"

Julian nodded.

Morrow said, "We go." The cab pulled back into the stream of traffic.

Julian's invasion of the Pentagon Building was a classic of its kind. The two Marine guards at the front portal didn't see him at all because they weren't looking for a small boy, holding a card in one hand, to march stolidly and unquestioningly between them and breach the main entrance. He had been decanted from Morrow's cab, but had left his suitcase behind, for when he had reached for his money to pay, Morrow had said simply, "Skip it, kid. I better be here when you come out and see what's next." Morrow had figured the boy for a maximum of probably five minutes before he would be ejected. No pass, no credentials, nothing but the personal card of a colonel in Ordnance, an address, an office telephone number and scribbled initials.

The lobby of the Pentagon presented the most efficient and complicated security check that could be devised by a nervous soldiery. There were counters, barriers, sergeants behind desks, Marine guards, military police and a smattering of officers.

Julian approached the nearest desk, behind which sat a Naval petty officer with six gold hash marks down his sleeve and two rows of ribbons.

He asked, "Please, sir, where can I find Colonel Sisson?"

The petty officer said, "Who's he?"

Julian showed him the card. The petty officer studied it and said, "Over there, sonny. Ask him," and indicated a corner of the lobby where everyone was khaki-clad.

Julian took his card to a sergeant at a desk and said again, "Please, sir, where can I find Colonel Sisson?"

The sergeant called over to another, "Hey, Joe, where's a Colonel John Sisson?"

Like a shuttlecock the name of Sisson was batted to and fro until it reached a corporal who was standing in front of a huge directory. He called back, "Southwest Wing, Corridor G, Second Floor, Room Nine Three Four. Colonel John G. Sisson. That right?"

The okays were wafted back by the same route. By the time they reached the desk of the original inquirer, the sergeant, Julian was no longer there.

He said, "Now, what the hell? Where did the kid go?" And then, as an important piece of brass with aiguillettes, shiny boots and an overloaded briefcase interrogated him, he forgot about Julian. The two guards at the inner entrance, seeing the boy leave the desk with the sergeant apparently satisfied, made no attempt to stop him. And thereafter, Julian, with the wing, the corridor, the floor and the room number firmly embedded in his mind, proceeded to penetrate the innermost recesses of the most protected building in the world.

A guard asked, "Have you got a pass?" Julian showed him the Colonel's card. The guard said, "Okay."

Another Cerberus asked the same question. Julian showed the card. The M.P. said, "That's no good. You've gotta have a pass."

Julian said, "The sergeant said it was okay."

"Which sergeant?"

"The one at the desk."

"Who? Billings? The fat guy?"

"Uh huh."

"Okay, go ahead."

The third was more adamant. "Nix, sonny. Nobody gets through here without a badge. Who sent you? How'd you get this far?"

Julian said, "But, Colonel Sisson's my . . ." He was going to say "friend," but a Marine at the inner portal impatiently finished it for him, grouching, "Oh, for Pete's sake. I wish the brass would let us know when their kids are coming. Go ahead and see your daddy, but don't say I let you through."

Julian said, "Gee thanks, that's swell."

The farther he went, the easier it seemed to be. Julian walked past two guards who never even questioned him and a third who seemed satisfied with his credential. He finally encountered two together who formed what appeared to be an impenetrable bulwark, for they wore sidearms and looked grim and impassable. But it turned out they were Army and quite the easiest, for one of them said, "Hey, you got yourself in the wrong corridor, sonny. C'mere, follow me. I'll show you where his office is." He led the way and in this manner Julian West arrived at the secretary's desk in the outer office of Colonel John G. Sisson, Weapons Department, United States Army Ordnance, and from thence was ushered into the presence of the senior sergeant guarding the portals of Major General Thomas Horgan.

The arguments and the row around the conference table in the General's office were not only still raging but had increased in scope and taken on a larger aspect, for the photograph of Nixon on the wall had cautioned Horgan, who was something of a safety-firster. He had called in a member of the President's Advisory Committee and acquainted him with such facts in the case as were available, should it blow up into something calling for diplomatic intervention and attention. In addition the State Department had contributed a pair of experts on Russian matters.

The newcomers, each seeing the affair from their own angles and bureaucratic fears, had solved nothing but had only managed to raise General Horgan's temperature beyond the boiling point, where he blew off at them collectively and individually.

". . . and all you can think about are your own goddamn jobs. Don't you ever give a thought to your country? I'm surrounded by a lot of horses' asses and stupid sons of bitches starting off with you, Sisson, and next whoever picked you for this job." He aimed a forefinger point blank at the unhappy Colonel and said, "You're gonna find yourself on the retired list so goddamn fast . . ."

At this point the General's sergeant, an old-timer whose length of service in the outer office entitled him to take liberties, entered, saluted, said, "I beg your pardon, General," and then going to Sisson, handed him a card.

He said, "Colonel, excuse me for busting in like this but there's a kid outside who knows you and says he has to see you on something important. I figured I better tell you because he got right through to your office without a pass. You know, we're supposed to have a lot of security around here and I thought maybe . . ."

Sisson took the card, mechanically turned it over and glanced at it. He saw his initials in his own handwriting and a cold chill took a long slide down his back as it brought up a memory of a bus ride, a boy and a diagram. Hardly daring to ask, he said, "He wouldn't be a four-eyed kid with red hair, a lot of freckles and a stammer, would he?"

The sergeant said, "He didn't have no stammer I could see."

In icy fury General Horgan addressed himself to the two men. "If you two are all through discussing what seems to be a family matter, will you oblige me, sergeant, by getting your ass out of here?"

The chill climbed back up Sisson's spine and raised the hackles on his neck. He thought, *No, no, that's impossible. I can't believe it. It's only in the movies that the Marines arrive in the nick of time.* Nevertheless aloud he said, "But, sir, may I . . ."

General Horgan blew again. To Sisson he shouted, "Shut up!" and to the sergeant he roared, "Get out!"

The sergeant did, but Julian entered as though on cue.

The room was still echoing to the General's bellows and Julian looked about him anxiously at the panoply of beribboned officers and grim-looking civilians gathered gloomily around the long conference table until he located Colonel Sisson. He went directly to him and said, "Excuse me, sir . . . I didn't mean . . . I guess I shouldn't have come in . . . I thought this was your office and you said, sir, that if I . . ."

Before he had finished Sisson had leaped up out of his chair and seized him by both shoulders. "Julian!"

All the roar had gone out of General Horgan and he was now so uptight that his voice had been reduced to a falsetto squeal as he inquired, "What the hell is going on here? I think I'm going to go out of my mind."

For all Sisson cared at that moment, the General's mind could go where it liked. He said, "Julian, have you still got that diagram?"

Julian replied, "Is it alright, sir? I mean, you said if I was in any trouble I should . . ."

The words came tumbling from Sisson, "Yes, yes, that's right. I did. That's exactly what I said and you were perfectly right to come. But your invention. You see, they'd all like to have a look at it."

It was considerably bewildering to Julian but still clear what the Colonel wanted and so he reached into his pocket and took out the grubby drawing of the Bubble Gun which Sisson unfolded and placed dramatically on the center of the conference table.

General Horgan had been just about to let out another

yell and now had to swallow the air he had drawn in for that purpose, causing his eyes to pop. He pointed a finger at the sheet of paper and managed to get out, "What's that thing?"

Sisson announced, "You said, sir, to produce the kid and his diagram, or else. Well, this is the kid, and that's the diagram," and then said to Julian, "Have you got the gun too?"

Julian reached into his pocket and produced it. Sisson laid it on the table. "And that's the gun," he added.

The two articles lay there hypnotizing the gaze of an entire section of the Intelligence and Diplomatic Service of the United States of America. Nobody seemed to be able to move.

An unidentified voice inquired in the stillness, "What time is it in Moscow?"

One of the Russian experts glanced at his watch. It was a quarter past eleven. He said, "Quarter past eight."

Another voice said, "Jesus," and then there was silence again.

General Tom Horgan now arose. He was, as a general should be, a huge, massive ex-football-playing figure, so powerful and bulky in his uniform as to give the impression of being undamageable by any existing type of military hardware. He leaned on his knuckles on the table, bent forward and scrutinized the diagram. The assemblage waited. Nobody said anything any more. Julian stood by Colonel Sisson and for a moment stared anxiously into his face. The Colonel did not know why but he was moved to put a protective arm about the boy's shoulder.

The General then reached forward and picked up the

Bubble Gun. Like every Ordnance man who ever lived, upon handling a pistol, he weighed it first in his palm and fitted it to his grip. He held it up to his eyes and examined it closely. He held it to his ear and shook it. Then, holding it at arm's length, he squeezed the trigger.

Before the horrified eyes of the experts, a soap bubble began to form at the muzzle. It expanded, inflated and grew until it was the size of a grapefruit, at which point it detached itself and, caught by the indirect lighting from the ceiling of the conference room, became exquisitely iridescent. It floated, changing colors. Ascending, it entered the stratum of the air-conditioning and on that current, before the fascinated eyes of the assemblage, it drifted straight for the watching portrait of Richard Milhous Nixon where it burst silently, leaving one tiny damp stain on the plate glass in the frame.

"HA!" burst from the lungs of General Horgan, and for a petrified moment, none of them knew whether this was the beginning of another bellow, a cry of anguish, or a sneeze, until it was followed by similar explosions, "HA HA HA HA HA!"

The General was laughing!

"HA HA HA HA HA HA!"

The table, the chairs and the whole room seemed to shake as he squeezed the trigger again and a whole stream of bubbles emerged.

And now the awful hypnotic spell was broken. The General was laughing; then laughter was permitted. They had all been bursting to let go and now they did and raised the roof with their shouts and screams, their yelps and yaks and bellows of merriment as the General

pounded the table with his fist in hysteric guffaws and
began to find words.

"Oh Jesus, Jesus, wait until the sons of bitches see this.
This is the funniest goddamn thing that ever happened.
Wait 'til they try to figure this one out. This is better than
anything we could have sent them. John, you're a goddamn hero even though you're a stupid bastard as well.
I'll get you a gong for this if it's the last thing I do. Oh,
brother, brother, I'd give my retirement pay if I could be
over there now, when they get a load of this."

The conference disintegrated, the friendly general was
slapping Sisson on the back. It wasn't only in the movies.
The Marines sometimes did arrive in the nick of time.

Julian thought they were all crazy.

In Moscow it was not a quarter past eight. It was a
quarter past seven, the Russian expert having been
wrong in his calculations. He usually was. In a conference room hidden away in a secret place on the edge of
the city were General Barzovsky, his staff and a collection
of experts from the KGB, MVD, and allied Intelligence,
Espionage and Counterespionage units.

The conference room was extraordinarily like the one
in the Pentagon Building, the same long polished table,
the same framed photograph looking down from the wall
except that there were two photographs instead of one,
Lenin, of course, and then the dour visage of Brezhnev.
The other difference was that the frame holding the
photograph of Brezhnev was so constructed that the top
could be removed and another photograph substituted
in a matter of seconds. But General Barzovsky appeared

just as huge and bullet-proof, square-headed and formi-
dable as General Horgan. The light glinted from polished black boots. Huge, blue-uniformed chests were
covered with medals and ribbons. The civilians wore
ill-fitting sack suits.

There was tension, high tension, in the room as the
assemblage awaited the fruition of years of planning and
preparation to lay their hands on what had been hinted
at as America's newest and most secret weapon. The spy
planted in the United States twelve years before to be
available for that one moment had succeeded in photographing it, a brilliant technician of the Soviet State had
succeeded in making a model. It was to be revealed.

General Barzovsky looked at his watch and rumbled,
"Well?"

A flustered aide also examined his watch and said nervously, "Any moment now, Comrade General. We have
had word that Comrade Uvanov is on his way here."

There was a stir at the door, murmurs, heel clicks, the
sound of passwords being demanded and given. The
entrance was impressive. A major in his greatcoat and
epaulettes; Comrade Uvanov, still in his laboratory over-
alls; and behind him Comrade Allon. Comrade Allon was
not entirely happy or comfortable for he was flanked by
two members of the Counterespionage group. The Major saluted and said, "Comrade General, here is Comrade Uvanov of the Special Engineering Branch, Comrade Allon of whom you have been told, and Comrades
Vishky and Rumov you know."

"Well?" rumbled General Barzovsky.

"Proceed," ordered the Major.

Comrade Uvanov threw a scrutable look at the Major for he was not entirely happy either but the officer was implacable and so the Ordnance engineer produced an enlarged photocopy of a diagram of the interior construction of a pistol, and likewise, made up from the diagram in black gunmetal and about the size of a .38 automatic, a model of the gun itself. This he laid upon the diagram in the center of the conference table. In the same deathly silence that had reigned only ten minutes before in the far-off Pentagon, those gathered around the table were semi-hypnotized.

General Barzovsky arose, likewise placed his knuckles upon the table, leaned forward and examined both articles.

"And what may I ask is that?" he said, indicating the diagram.

The Major clicked off the reply as though by rote, "It is a photograph of the diagram of the latest secret weapon of the Department of Ordnance of the United States Army obtained by Comrade Allon."

"And that?" inquired the General.

"That," replied the Major, "is a working model of the secret weapon itself achieved by the skill of Comrade Uvanov with the aid of the obviously coded instructions to be found on the photograph. And here, Comrade General, may I put in a word for the genius of Comrade Maranovsky of our decoding department who broke the code by discovering that it was not a code at all, but actual instructions for manufacture of the weapon thus bringing to naught the brilliance of the American scheme to confuse us."

General Barzovsky once more regarded the diagram and then he looked over Comrades Uvanov, Allon and the Major and all those sitting about the table in silence, and the expression upon his face was of one looking at the insane.

He reached over now and took the diagram in his left hand and the gun in his right. He went through the ritual of examination, then dropped the diagram back onto the table and, holding the pistol at arm's length, squeezed the trigger. A grapefruit-sized bubble formed faithfully at the nozzle, detached itself and floated away and then another and another and a fourth and fifth as the General kept squeezing. They were all of the same size for the Comrade Engineer had constructed the model from the penciled corrections made by Colonel Sisson rather than from Julian's original. This Bubble Gun was working perfectly. The bubbles that filled the air of the conference room were even more beautiful than those that had entertained the Pentagon group for in place of indirect lighting there was a huge central crystal chandelier. The building formerly had belonged to the Chief of Staff of the Army of His Most Holy Majesty, the Czar of All the Russias. The crystals of the chandelier broke the light into all the colors of the rainbow and the bubbles caught them up magnificently and floated away with them to burst here and there wherever they alighted before the horrified gaze of the onlookers.

In a way it was as though the General himself was hypnotized for he did not seem to be able to stop squeezing the trigger and producing more bubbles. Not all of them exploded, Russian soap apparently was tougher than the American brand. Some settled upon heads or shoulders, others came to rest on the backs of chairs or on the table. One rose briefly into the air and then returned and settled comfortably upon the hand of General Barzovsky where it reflected him expanded fivefold in the manner of one of the mirrors in a fun fair before it blew up quietly and in doing so broke the spell for the General, for he put the gun back onto the table, sat down, raised one ham of a fist and thundered it down upon the wood while from his massive chest there burst the most tremendous "HO!"

Comrade Allon quietly slid to the floor in a dead faint for there was nothing for him but the firing squad and thus he missed the second and third "HO's!" which burst from the General to startle and surprise the trembling gathering as "HO!" after "HO!" flowed and tears streamed from the General's eyes. He was laughing his head off.

He was laughing. General Barzovsky was laughing. He was not angry, infuriated, maddened with rage, he was pleased to be amused. Then it was permitted for everyone to laugh and so shouts and screams and yells and bellows went up to join the hilarity of a Russian general with a sense of humor until the last of the bubbles exploded into nothingness and the crystal pendants of the great chandelier tinkled against one another stirred by the waves of laughter.

15

Julian asked, "What happened?"

They were in Sisson's office. The sergeant, sitting at his desk, was still grinning to himself. The story had circulated. The Colonel rocked back in his swivel chair. On his desk before him was Julian's diagram and the Bubble Gun. He likewise indulged in a reflective smile before he replied.

"It's too complicated, Julian." And then feeling that this was unfair and on the short side, he said, "Often when men get into a panic over some things and become nervous and fearful, and fear that all is getting out of control, they react to the situation by doing something silly in the hope that what it is that is worrying them will get distracted and go away."

Julian, in his straight-backed chair, the soles of his Keds barely meeting the carpeting, stared. The explanation was not being all that explanatory.

"Well," the Colonel continued, "due to an accident of circumstances and thanks to you as well, something sillier than usual happened and everybody is very pleased with me, and I shall be eternally grateful to you."

"Me?" Julian cried. "What did I do?"

The Colonel did not reply immediately. Then, he said gravely, "As I told you before, Julian, it's a little too difficult to explain, but I want you to make me a promise, will you?"

Behind their lenses, Julian's eyes grew larger.

The Colonel then said, "About anything you saw or heard in that room you keep your lip buttoned."

Julian was momentarily rendered speechless by the tremendous import of the Colonel's warning, but even better was to come.

"Here," added the Colonel and opening a drawer of his desk, he extracted a rubber stamp and ink pad and applied the former to the latter. Then, he reached over and carefully pressed the stamp first upon Julian's diagram and then upon the back of the boy's hand. In glorious purple ink it read TOP SECRET.

"Get it?" the Colonel asked.

Julian looked upon the mark on his hand as though he had been awarded the Congressional Medal and, without realizing it, raised it and held it momentarily to his cheek where it made a faint purple smudge. Then he whispered, "Yes, sir. I wouldn't say anything to anyone, ever."

The marvel of what Colonel Sisson had done all but

totally stifled his curiosity, but once again he felt the sweet inner thrill of having participated, of having in a mysterious way come close to something important, exciting and even dangerous in the world of grownups. The words TOP SECRET confirmed this. For the moment it was sufficient to have been told in this manner that he and his Bubble Gun had again played a part that this time was too tremendous even to be talked about. That was the way things were between men.

The Colonel asked, "How did you make out at the Patent Office?"

The exquisite feeling drained from Julian's breast, the glare of reality chased the shadows of his fantasy and he was back once more in the world of real trouble. He would have been glad to have relieved himself in tears but not in front of Colonel Sisson or the sergeant who was now writing on some papers with one hand and at the same time listening with both ears.

Instead Julian simply shook his head in silent negation, delved into his pocket and produced a pink pamphlet from the United States Department of Commerce entitled, "Patents and Inventions, an Information Aid for Inventors." The Colonel took it and regarded it gloomily.

He sighed, "I know it practically by heart."

"Oh," said Julian, "do you invent . . . ?"

The Colonel nodded, "In one way or another."

Julian remained silent and the Colonel leafed through the pamphlet. He opened it apparently at random and in a low voice began to mutter a long extract of instructions, which Julian already had heard via Mr. Morrow.

The Colonel droned on: " 'One inch from its edges a single marginal line is to be drawn, leaving the "sight" precisely 8 by 13 inches. Within this margin all work must be included. One of the shorter sides of the sheet is regarded as its top, and, measuring down from the marginal line, a space of not less than 1¼ inches is to be left blank for the heading of title, name, number and date, which will be applied by the Office in a uniform style.' " He paused and interpolated, "God, bureaucrats. Listen to this. 'Character of lines: All drawings must be made with drafting instruments or by photolithographic process which will give them satisfactory reproduction characteristics. Every line and letter (signatures included) must be absolutely black. This direction applies to all lines however fine, to shading, and to lines representing cut surfaces in sectional views. All lines must be clean, sharp and solid, and fine or crowded lines should be avoided. Solid black should not be used for sectional or surface shading. Freehand work should be avoided wherever it is possible to do so.' "

When he had finished he looked over the edge of the pamphlet at Julian, who was regarding him miserably.

"Uh huh," said the Colonel. "I tried to give you an idea on the bus. Did they tell you about researching?"

Julian nodded in the affirmative.

The Colonel continued, ". . . and recommend that you acquire a practitioner—a patent attorney?"

Julian nodded again.

"Did you see an examiner?" But the Colonel shook his head and answered his own question. "No, you wouldn't until you'd filed your drawing and claim and paid your fee. Well . . ." He leafed through the pamphlet again and looking up at Julian saw that his lips and chin were trembling and that he had better do something about it.

He said, "Look here, Julian, it isn't as bad as all that. It actually sounds a lot worse than it is. Anyway, what we can do is fix you up with your first step, the drawing. I'll have one of my draftsmen get on it right away. We could have it ready for you by tomorrow morning. You could take it over to the Patent Office, file it and then see what would happen."

"Gee, sir, would you?" It came out almost as a shout of delight and gratitude, but immediately after his face clouded over.

He said, "The filing fee. The sixty-five dollars. They told me about it. I haven't got it. I spent almost all my money getting here."

Sisson nodded gravely. "Hmmmm, I see, that would be a problem. Look here, would you let me give . . . ?"

Julian was positive and immediate, "Oh, no, sir, I couldn't. I wanted to make my own money to show my dad."

"Show your dad what?"

Julian considered. Here they were again, always with their grownup questions that had to be answered somehow. He replied, "That my invention would work. He didn't care. I mean, I guess he didn't think it would or anything."

The Colonel, reflecting for a moment, wondered about the boy's father and what he was like and what truth there had been in everything which at one time or another Julian had told him, and then he thought about himself being a father too and up popped instances where he could have been too short with answers to his son or daughter. How could one ever really know with youngsters?

He said, "Julian, have you any idea of the hook you got me off? Would you let me lend it to you?"

"How could I pay you back?"

"Royalties from your patent."

Julian was still doubtful. He said, "Sir, what if somebody else got there first? The man said it would have to be looked up."

Sisson smiled. "In that case, the government, in its benevolence, returns your filing fee. You could give me a note. Here, I'll fix it up."

He took a pen and a sheet of paper, speaking as he wrote, "I, Julian West, of—" He looked up. "What was your address again?" Julian gave it to him. "Promise to pay Colonel John Sisson, on demand, the sum of sixty-five dollars." He counted out the money from a billfold and handed it over. "There, now, you sign it and it's all correct and legal. It's a loan and you're under no further obligation." At the same time he handed back the Bubble Gun and said, "Here, we won't be needing this."

"That's terrific, sir. Thank you very much. What time do you think the drawing will be ready?"

"Say ten o'clock tomorrow morning."

Julian said, "I'll come back for it, sir."

The Colonel looked up and made an assumption. He said, "Oh, then you've got a place to stay."

Julian said nothing. It was the Colonel's assertion, not his. He didn't wish to burden the Colonel any further.

He thought he had enough money left for a cheap room somewhere. The cab driver could help him find one.

The Colonel picked up the diagram again and glanced over it. He said, "Hang on a sec while I have a word with my assistant about the changes. I want to be sure." He left the office to return a few minutes later to find his sergeant alone in the office.

"Hello," he said, "where's the boy?"

The sergeant replied, "He said he'd be back in the morning."

The Colonel looked puzzled for a moment, then glanced at the note that Julian had signed. He no longer had the diagram, which he had turned over to a draftsman. He thought for a moment and then said to his sergeant, "Get me a Mr. West at 137 East View Terrace, San Diego, California, on the phone."

The sergeant balked. He said, "Aw, look here, sir, you ain't gonna give him away, are you? That's the kid who was in the papers with the hijacker on the bus. I recognized him."

The Colonel said, "Well, if you read the papers then you ought to realize that by now his parents must be frantic what with his disappearance and all that. Put the call through. By the time his father gets here it'll be morning, the kid will have his drawing and be at the Patent Office. Mission accomplished."

It had been a good hour since Julian had vanished into the interior of the Pentagon. Meech Morrow had slumped a little into his seat and was talking to himself. "Boy, you're sure one smart cab driver. I'll bet they must have got on to the kid and are holding him to send home to his folks and you got yourself about nine dollars worth of nothing on the clock besides wasting half the day. Wait 'til I tell Mother about Meech Morrow, the great philanthropist . . ." At this point Julian emerged from the doorway ten feet tall and beaming.

Morrow sat up blinking and then said, "Julian, I mean, Herman, what happened?"

Julian said, "Say, the Colonel was okay. They're gonna make me the design and everything and there were a whole lot of generals sitting around yakking. I gotta be back at ten o'clock in the morning."

Meech Morrow was a normal man who liked things to make sense. This did not. But then nothing had since the time he had encountered Julian, including his own behavior. He said, "Come on, now, what really happened? What was it all about? Let's quit kidding. You're the boy that shot that hijacker with your little old water pistol, aren't you?"

Julian said, "It wasn't a water pistol. It was my Bubble Gun, my invention, and the Colonel said . . ." Thereupon he remembered and continued, "I'm not allowed to say. Look!" and he exhibited the back of his hand to Morrow.

The cab driver stared and then grinned. "Top Secret, are you?" He said, "Well, you won't be for long with every cop in town on the lookout for you. What are you going to do now?"

Julian stared at Morrow without replying. He hadn't thought.

Morrow said, "You haven't got any place to go, have you?"

Julian shook his head and admitted it, "No."

It dawned suddenly upon Morrow that although things like a nine-year-old boy fugitive from San Diego trying to patent a pistol that shot bubbles instead of bullets wasn't exactly the normal run of affairs, neither was the story in the newspapers about a hijacking and, whatever, Julian was not a liar. There had been the Colonel's card in his pocket and if Julian said the Colonel was going to have his drawing and everything and to come back at ten in the morning, well by then the drawing and everything would be there. Aloud he said to Julian, "Look here, you better come along home with me or you won't be making it to any Patent Office in the morning. And just to keep it strictly business let's say you pay me off now. That'll be nine dollars and a half."

Julian handed him a ten-dollar bill. Morrow asked, "Okay I keep the fifty-cent tip?"

Julian nodded, "Uh huh."

Morrow said, "Right! then get in."

Julian opened the back door, but Morrow said, "No, no, up front here with me. From now on, Julian, you're my guest."

The race to the wire, on the face of it, appeared to be unfair and staked against Julian who at 2:30 in the afternoon of that day was finishing lunch with Mrs. Morrow and the baby, the other two Morrow children, a boy and a girl, being at school. And, at exactly the same hour Frank Marshall was opening the door of one of the inner offices of the drafting firm of Peabody and Wilson to find the draftsman waiting for him with a grin on his face and the drawing ready.

The draftsman said, "Here you are. Have you worked out the rest of the forms?"

Marshall exhibited the sheaf of papers. The draftsman said, "You getting a patent attorney—a practitioner?"

Marshall said, "Can't afford to. I'm down to my last five C's."

The draftsman tapped the beautiful inked design. He said, "You can't afford not to. This is a pretty simple little idea. You'd better have someone who knows his way about and can give you protection. They'll run you ragged over there if you try to push this through by yourself. Go to Shine, Williams and Burdett on the eighth floor and ask for Jim Williams. Say I sent you. They're reasonable and won't sting you. Here, I'll give you my card." He scribbled a few words on a business card and gave it to Marshall.

Jim Williams was a fat, pursy little man but he had vivid, alert and intelligent eyes and a brisk manner.

"I'm in a hurry," Marshall began.

And Williams said, "Yes, yes, I know," and glanced at his watch. He then said, "Two hundred bucks retainer. If the patent is denied it won't cost you any more. If it's granted, another three hundred. What you want to do is get this in before closing. I know all the examiners over there." And he was on his way out of the office with Marshall trooping after him.

Two hundred dollars was pretty steep, but at least Williams was a hustler. At twenty minutes past four they were in the office of an examiner and Frank Marshall's papers had been dated and time-stamped as well as given a registry number, and Marshall had further been relieved of his sixty-five-dollar filing fee. The examiner and the lawyer then exchanged some gobbledygook after which Williams told Marshall, "There's some more processing before we start the search, but it's too late this afternoon. We can come back tomorrow morning and get it done. Anyway," and he indicated the stamps and numbers on the material, "you're registered as of now, so you can sleep tonight."

Walking down the corridor to the exit, for the first time Frank Marshall found himself wondering whether he could sleep.

16

At 10:15 the following morning, for
the second time Julian emerged from
the imposing portals of the Pentagon
Building except that this time he was
accompanied by Colonel Sisson. Meech
Morrow's cab was faithfully drawn up at
the curb behind the black Cadillac
limousine belonging to a one-star
General. A sergeant sat at the driver's
wheel.

Sisson said, "There you are, young
man. A General's car. How does that
suit you? Everything in style."

Julian thought that he would die of
excitement. He said, "Say, gee, for me?
How did you . . . ?"

Colonel Sisson said smoothly,

"Borrowed it. He was only too delighted. The driver will look after you."

The sergeant was around and holding the door open. The scene was almost grotesque in its absurdity, the great car, the smartly uniformed officer and the rumpled little boy.

Sitting in his cab Meech Morrow grinned to himself and wondered whether Julian would remember.

He did. Julian suddenly cried, "Oh say, excuse me," and he ran over to the cab. The Colonel sauntered after him. Julian said, "Look, Mr. Morrow, I'm going in a General's car."

Morrow nodded and said, "I see that. I guess you're in good hands. You won't be needing me any more."

Julian was aware that the Colonel was standing beside them and said, "Mr. Morrow here looked after me. I stayed with him last night."

The Colonel nodded and said, "So that's where you were. I wondered," bent down to the driver and said, "That was very kind of you, Mr. Morrow," and then added, "Do we owe you anything?" And having asked it, he wished he hadn't.

But Morrow was not offended. He merely said, "No sir, thank you, nobody owes me anything. He's a great kid. We were proud to have him in our home."

Julian held out his hand and said, "Thanks, Mr. Morrow, and thank Mrs. Morrow again too, please."

Morrow nodded, held the small hand for a moment, then eased his car into gear. "Good luck, kid, and you might let me know how things turn out."

Julian said, "Yes sir, I will," as the car moved off and

Colonel Sisson gave him a goodbye salute. And it wasn't until it turned the corner out of sight that he realized he had not asked Morrow for his address, which he had failed to observe.

An hour later Julian sat in a straight-backed government utility chair in the office of an examiner of applications for patents in the United States Patent Office. On the desk lay an expertly and properly executed drawing of the diagram of the Bubble Gun plus the various forms filled out carefully and neatly in Julian's large print in which he had been aided by Meech Morrow's wife who had been a school teacher. Each sheet was in proper order including the receipt for the sixty-five-dollar filing fee. The examiner leafed through these and several times during his inspection, looked up at Julian rather sharply. Yet this no longer brought any fear to Julian. He had become used to it, this look of people trying to remember where they had seen him before. But now it no longer mattered. He was at the end of his quest, at least the part which had come to mean the most, the patenting of his invention.

He was a wiser boy and wasted no time in regrets over his former innocence or even the manner in which he had embarked upon his voyage, and the dreams and the golden fantasies of millions of dollars with which it had been colored. These would be entertained again but one of the things he had learned was that first things come first. A patent granted to him for his Bubble Gun would be something to show his father.

The examiner indeed had been wondering what was familiar about this boy but the problems which were posed by these papers before him and the subsequent happenings quickly drove this thought from his mind.

He leafed through the papers again, picked them up in a bunch and once more laid them down on his desk. Then he asked, "Where did you get these? You did say these drawings were original?"

Julian replied, "Yes sir. It's my Bubble Gun. I invented it, but the drawings were made by a friend of mine in the Pentagon Building. Are they okay?"

The examiner looked at Julian even more sharply now. He repeated, "The Pentagon Building. I don't understand."

Julian said, "Colonel Sisson. He's a friend of mine. I didn't have the right kind of paper or ink or anything and so he said . . ." He then bethought himself of something which would surely put an end to this line of questioning and reached into his pocket. "But here's *my* diagram."

The official took it and examined it, comparing it with the work done by the draftsman. He asked, "What's this TOP SECRET stamp on it?"

For the first time since the triumphant parade of happy events that had led him to this point, Julian had a momentary feeling of alarm. He replied, "I'm not allowed to say."

The examiner inquired, "Is this an Army job? Who's this Colonel Sisson?"

Julian had his precious card which had opened so many doors for him and he produced it. The examiner took it, looked at it and copied it down on a pad. Then he asked, holding up the draftsman's sheet, "Why isn't the TOP SECRET stamp on this one as well then? I don't

get it." And then he looked at Julian even more questioningly, as his eye caught the words on the back of Julian's
hand. Mrs. Morrow had wanted to wash it off the night
before, but Julian had refused to let her. He was never
going to wash it off. He had been careful to soap and dry
only the palm.

For a moment the examiner found himself bewildered.
TOP SECRET on the identical diagram, TOP SECRET on the
boy's hand, a colonel of Ordnance in the Pentagon!
What kind of kid stuff or foolishness was involved? The
immediate escape hatch from what seemed to be some
kind of nonsense was the return strictly to business
which was what he was being paid for.

He therefore turned to Julian and said, "Actually,
young fellow, a complete duplicate set of these drawings
and applications passed through my office late yesterday
afternoon. They're probably being processed right now.
Here, wait a minute, let me have a look."

He got up from his desk and went out into the corridor. Julian slipped down off his chair and followed him.
He had only half understood what the man had been
saying. Perhaps it was only something to do with the
formalities, something perhaps that had escaped him or
Colonel Sisson. Yet he could feel his heart thumping
violently in his chest.

As he and the examiner emerged from the office, almost at the same moment, about three down, a door
opened and to his complete astonishment and bewilderment, Julian saw Marshall accompanied by a fat, busy
little man, and another who was obviously an official and
was saying to the fat man, "That's all okay, Jim. You

know where to go now. Third floor, second office on the right. They'll look after you."

Julian's lips formed the word "Frank" but no sound issued and he was aware that he was suddenly horribly frightened.

Julian's examiner was saying to the other official, "Oh, Fred, see here, wait a minute. Here's something pretty funny. I've got an identical set of plans for that same invention presented by this kid as his own. What goes on here? Can we have a look?"

The official said, "Yeah, sure, why, what's wrong?" The two groups moved closer to one another.

The sudden, unexpected appearance of his friend had set up not only an inexplicable fear in Julian but a total confusion of thoughts, bewilderments, explanations.

It *was* Frank Marshall. Frank Marshall, his pal. It couldn't be anybody else. There was the handsome, stalwart figure, the worn battle jacket with the spots where the ribbons, shoulder patches and chevrons had been removed and those unforgettable bright blue half-mocking, half-friendly eyes. What was it that had happened? Of course. He had gone to make a telephone call at the terminal and then they had managed to lose one another in the crowd. Any other possibility but the one that now followed in Julian's mind was unacceptable and he was suddenly flooded with relief because of what he chose to believe. Of course. Marshall knew that he, Julian, would be at the Patent Office and naturally this would be where he would come to find him.

Julian said, "We got lost, didn't we? When you didn't come out I went into the station to look for you but I couldn't find you anywhere."

Frank Marshall did not reply. It was as though he had not heard. And then Julian noticed that now those bright blue eyes were neither friendly nor mocking but stony cold as they stared over the top of his head.

Julian's examiner said to Marshall, "Do you know this boy?"

Marshall replied, "Who, the kid? Never saw him before in my life."

One stricken cry emerged from Julian, "But, Frank!"

Marshall turned his back. The examiner said to the other official, "Can I see those papers a minute again, Fred?" He took them and gave them a cursory glance and said, "That's right, those are the ones," and handed them back.

The official said, "They came through last night just before closing. We decided to process them this morning."

"Yes, thanks, I know. They're the ones I accepted yesterday."

Marshall turned to his group and said, "Okay?"

The official nodded and the fat man took the papers.

Marshall said, "Then, let's go."

Julian watched them go off down the corridor. He felt sick. As from a far distance he heard the examiner say, "Well, that seems to be that. Suppose we go back to my office for a minute, sonny, and have a little chat."

Numbly Julian followed him and then he was once more propped up in the straight-backed chair and the distant voice was saying, "If you say this is original with you, young man, I have to take your word for it. I've been in this office long enough to see duplicate inventions submitted but never anything like this. However, it's none of my business."

Julian simply sat quietly, like one paralyzed, his eyes seeing the man, his ears hearing him but his thoughts now ranging far in search of the answer to the impossible. How could Marshall have done this? When could he have, and above all, why? His friend. The diagram had never left his pocket or person until he handed it over to Colonel Sisson. Where? When? How? The roster of cities passed through his mind. St. Louis, Indianapolis, Columbus, but they had always been together sauntering through the bus stations during the stopovers. What was it he half remembered then? Where was it? Pittsburgh. And as a long-ago nighttime dream recalled, it seemed to Julian that he had been asleep and there had been a shadow that had fallen across him and a touch and then he had slept the more deeply and the more peacefully because it would have been surely the friendly, comforting pressure of Frank Marshall's hand upon his shoulder. He had awakened an hour or so after they had left Pittsburgh.

The man was still talking. "I'll accept this application if you like, but I think it's only fair to tell you that you'd be wasting your time and money. The one you saw go down the hall is time-stamped as having been received yesterday and the serial number is twenty-seven ahead of yours. In other words, if the research proves it patentable, it will always have priority. I can't say I was overly impressed with that young man there and if there was any funny business, I suppose you could sue. What about your family? Have you got a father or someone?"

He looked up at Julian and then down at the papers again. Julian was unable to reply. The chill that began at his feet seemed to have moved up, gripping his middle.

The examiner said, "Wait a minute, I just had an idea. Did you ever make a model of your invention?"

Julian nodded in assent.

"Well, that's something. Have you got it?"

Julian moved his head in negation.

"Where is it, then?"

"I gave it to the baby."

"Eh? Gave it to . . . what baby?"

"The taxi man's baby. The one where I stayed last night. He wanted it."

It seemed to Julian as though one part of him had been turned to ice, no longer flesh and blood capable of thought or movement, but yet there was another part that could remember, and in some recess of his mind he heard again the baby's gurgle of delight as the jet stream of bubbles emerged from the muzzle of the Bubble Gun and went sailing about the Morrow apartment the night before, sticking here, there and everywhere on bits of furniture and one even on the end of the baby's nose. When the baby had reached for it, it had disappeared, leaving him with the mystery of a droplet in his palm.

The baby's name was Matthew, he was a year and a half old and sat in a high chair. Julian had had the most fabulous dinner, ham steak with candied yams and peas and apple pie and cheese.

There was Della, the daughter, aged twelve, and Tom, the boy of fifteen and Abbie, Mrs. Morrow, who Julian thought had the most beautiful face of anyone he had ever seen. It was hard to tell why it was so beautiful except that when she looked at you it made you feel good all the way through, and happy.

After supper Julian had had to re-enact the shooting of the hijacker for the benefit of all, which he had then performed after suitable protestations that, "Aw, it was nothing," which Julian somehow knew was obligatory to prefacing an account of any extraordinary deed. Meech Morrow played the hijacker, Tom took the part of the bus driver, Matthew screamed with delight, Della applauded and Abbie Morrow had looked upon the boy with wonder and admiration.

Afterwards, Julian had been bedded down on the couch in the living room–dining room and Mrs. Morrow had covered him with a blanket and dropped a featherlike kiss upon his cheek. Morrow had looked in and ordered, "Now, you go to sleep. Don't worry, I'll get you up in the morning and we'll be back at the Pentagon at ten o'clock."

Replete and drowsy, Julian had murmured, "Thank you for everything, Mr. Morrow. Gee, that was a great supper."

And in the morning he had filled the soapy solution compartment of the Bubble Gun for the last time and presented it to the baby as the only thank-you gift he felt he could leave behind. And as he went out through the door with Morrow, the last thing he saw was the iridescence of a bubble floating across the room and the last thing he heard was the laughter of Matthew.

The examiner suddenly felt himself on the verge of losing his temper. He repeated, "The taxi man's baby wanted it? What are you talking about, boy? What taxi man? Where was all this?"

The part of Julian that was still able to function replied, "I don't know, sir, I can't remember where it was."

The examiner recovered his temper, for in a curious way something of Julian's state of mind had managed to penetrate to him. There was more behind this curious mix-up and the strange encounter in the hall. That man who denied ever having seen a boy who had called him by his first name. But, whatever it was, the official now wanted to be quit of it and with a sigh of defeat and resignation, he said, "I'm afraid I can't help you then, but it's up to you now, my boy." He picked up the sheaf of papers and held them so Julian could take them if he wished.

He asked, "Well, what do you want to do, take them back or leave them?"

The numbness had set in upon Julian again, the feeling that something inside him had died, that even some part of his body no longer belonged to him. He arose from the chair and without taking the papers, turned and went out.

He found his way down the corridor and a flight of steps to the lobby where there was a marble bench and he sat down on it leaning his back against a pillar, listening but not hearing the shuffle of the feet of passing people. He was still in a state of shock and unaware that in his right hand he held the mussed and grubby original diagram of the Bubble Gun which the examiner had returned to him. Dry-eyed, he remained sitting there staring at nothing.

Julian did not see Frank Marshall as he emerged from the bank of elevators behind him, but Marshall caught sight out of the corner of his eye of the small figure dwarfed even more by the marble pillar. He kept on going. In this manner, he had snatched no more than a camera shutter's glimpse at a fraction of a second of the child's face, of which he did not wish to be reminded. For already, indelibly imprinted on his memory was Julian in the corridor just a while ago when he had denied him. He would never be able to obliterate the look of incomprehension and bewilderment. Hitting a baby was one of the thoughts that had crossed Marshall's mind, and then a little later when he had had time to think he went all the way back to his Sunday school days and wondered what had been the expression upon the face of Christ when Peter had denied him.

And yet he knew that it was necessary to be strong, strong and tough. In today's jungle you had to look out for Number One! The patent lawyer had been sanguine about the chances of the invention. Marshall had no way of knowing that patent lawyers were always sanguine.

As he made for the revolving door, and his exit forever from the life and times of Julian West, inventor, Marshall felt himself yanked to a stop as though someone had flung a lasso about his shoulders and hauled it taut, bringing him to a standstill.

Yet, of course, nothing of the kind had happened. He was simply rooted in front of the revolving door which was going bump-bump-thumpety-thump as turning upon its axis it let people in and others out, all except Frank Marshall who suddenly was unable to move or even twitch so much as a muscle to join them.

One half revolution through that door and before him would lie freedom. Behind him—? Frank Marshall slowly turned about to punish himself with one last look at what he was leaving so that always it would remain with him.

He had not thought that it would be quite so dreadful or shattering. He had expected tears or abject misery but not the look of one whom shock and disillusionment had robbed of every aspect of childhood and had left nothing but a caricature.

His feet thought for him, for to his surprise he found that they were turning inexorably away from the door and wholly without his volition proceeding one behind the other until they brought him up standing, towering over Julian and looking down upon the little figure.

The child did not look up. The two legs that had come to a halt before him meant nothing. Nothing would ever mean anything again.

Marshall squatted down, hunkering upon his heels, and this brought his face level with that of the boy. He heard himself say "Julian," and realized that he was still under that same spell that had seized and paralyzed him at the door. But the way he spoke the name made Julian turn his head slightly so that Marshall was confronted with the full force of the white, stricken face.

Marshall said in a voice he hardly recognized as his own, "Okay, kid, so I'm a rat."

Julian stared at him, a flicker of life was returning to the eyes behind the lenses of the spectacles but he remained silent.

The Frank Marshall that knew he simply had to explain and in some manner drive that terrible dead look of an old and beaten man from the face of the boy, made his attempt to explain.

He said, "Look, I guess maybe you won't understand and it's tough when you get a real kick in the pants, but see, it's like this. You're young, you're a sort of a genius. You've got a great head on you. You're gonna invent a whole lot of other things besides the Bubble Gun." He paused and his voice dropped a note lower and he wished he could turn his head away as he added, "But right now, Julian, I need it more than you do."

Their eyes, on a level, were caught up. Julian said nothing.

Marshall continued, "See, I put my last buck down for that patent. No kidding. You know, all those drawings and stuff cost money. I suppose you got the Colonel to do it for you. I'm flat on my—" He had started to say "flat on my ass," but cleaned it up quickly to, "I'm flat broke, but I can get some sort of a job to keep myself going and when the patent goes through I'll have a stake. See? I could get a real start."

If only the boy would do or say something or burst into tears or poke a grimy fist into his eye, lash out at him, instead of this dead, cold and still uncomprehending stare.

Yet it was not entirely uncomprehending for Marshall was too uncomfortable and guilt ridden to see that something was awakening behind the lenses of the spectacles.

He pleaded, "Look, kid, we had a great time together, didn't we? And I kept the cops off your back, didn't I? You got your picture in the papers, you're a hero and when you get back to school all the kids will be envious of you."

For the first time then Marshall became aware that something had been stirring in Julian and that he was being studied by him. The boy's face was no longer dead but only perplexed and questioning. For a moment Marshall didn't know which was worse, the dead boy or the one come to life, and what that one would say.

He got in quickly with, "You know you had plenty of guts going off like you did not knowing anything about, well, you know—and you weren't scared like me of that hijacker, were you?" And this last brought up the scene again and something that had been missing and so after a moment's hesitation he said, "Do you want to let me have the gun? See, you wouldn't be needing it now and they asked me about it upstairs."

Automatically, Julian's hand went to the pocket where the Bubble Gun used to live. Marshall's eyes followed the gesture. Julian was shaking his head slowly in negation as his hand came out of his pocket empty, pulling a part of the lining with it. Then Marshall knew that for whatever reason he no longer had the Bubble Gun, but that if he had he would have given it to him. And it was Marshall and not Julian at that moment who fought back tears.

He said, "What else can I say, kid? Maybe in a way it's a good lesson for afterwards. Never trust anybody, especially a guy like me."

He rose to his feet, but remained gazing down saying, "I'll let you know how things come out," and then after another moment's hesitation, "No hard feelings, eh, Julian?"

Julian looked dumbly and miserably into Marshall's eyes and slowly shook his head. This was the most pain-

ful and astonishing thing of all he had to endure, to show
that he understood and that there were no hard feelings.
He felt nothing but a deep and unappeasable sorrow that
only the young can experience, the grief of disillusionment and the shattering of trust.

Marshall held out his hand and asked, "Will you
shake?"

Slowly Julian put a limp hand into Marshall's and they
shook. Marshall found he could bear it no longer. He had
wanted to finish with something like "Good luck, kid,"
but was unable to bring it out. Instead, he gave the cold
hand one more squeeze, turned quickly away, strode
across the lobby and plunged through the revolving
door, thus affording that Fate which looks after matters
of absurd timing her daily giggle. For as Marshall went
out through one side of the door, Aldrin West came in
the other.

For a moment West paused inside, confused by the
traffic shuffling through the lobby, and then almost immediately spied his son and hurried over to him.

"Julian, my God, I'm glad I've found you."

The meeting, of course, was like nothing he had expected or imagined. He had seen himself throwing his
arms about the boy and hugging him hard and Julian
perhaps glad to see him and returning the embrace. He
was not prepared for the rather diffident and quiet person who looked up at him from the bench, his face almost
expressionless and his voice oddly muted as he greeted
him with "Hello, Dad."

His father sat down beside him. He said, "Julian, I've
seen the Colonel. I've just come from there. He told me

all about you. I'm proud of you. And everything that was
in the newspapers about what you did. You're the greatest son a man ever had and I've been a rotten father to
you."

Julian looked surprised at this and even shook his head
slightly in negation for he had never really thought so.
It had never dawned upon him to evaluate his father, or
even his mother, as good, bad or indifferent. Parents
were as they were and that was that.

Julian said, "No, you aren't . . ." But then suddenly his
voice trailed off. He stopped and the strange faraway
look with which West was to become familiar passed into
his eyes again.

West said, "Your idea is great, you know. It'll work.
The Colonel said so."

But the look upon Julian's face had become so remote
and bleak that West became alarmed. He said, "Has
something gone wrong? What happened? Have you filed
the papers? Look, now that I'm here I can help you. The
Colonel explained about getting an attorney . . ."

Julian, deep down, had been glad and comforted by
seeing his father and having him there, but now all the
sadness arising from what had happened to him heaved
like a tide within Julian and forced him to shake his head
again. He began, "They were stol—somebody got there
ahead of me. I was too late."

17

They were on the jet plane side by side,
Julian in the window seat, homeward
bound. He had told his father the story
piecemeal, except for the Top Secret
part, interrupted by long silences which
were puzzling to Aldrin West but which
because of his new-found respect for
his son he did not attempt to penetrate.
West felt that there was more than the
talked-about generation gap between
himself and his son. There was a
mystery connected with Julian of which
the father was strongly aware. Perhaps
it had always been present in some
degree or other, lying behind the
puzzle that Julian had refused to be an
image of himself, to his annoyance. But
now the father was sensitive to the fact

that there was something deeper and that although his son had appeared glad to see him and was content to return home West felt himself cut off, closed out and unable to penetrate into what had really happened. There had been the newspaper account, there had been Julian's story and there was still the enigma—Julian.

The pain within Julian was always there. A deep and unhealing wound and it seemed that every part of the story that he had told to his father or the questions he answered were in some way attached to this wound and kept tugging at it and hurting him. Marshall, Marshall, Marshall!

Childhood was over. Julian stood on the threshold of young man, with all the pangs of adolescence still to be suffered. He was, therefore, totally unable to talk about such things as love and pain even if he could have put his emotions into words. Most difficult of all, in fact almost impossible, was for Julian to synthesize, understand and separate the dual nature of his hurt, stemming not only from what had been done to him, but from that last meeting where his friend had laid himself so horribly bare, the glimpse Julian had had as well of what it was that Marshall had done to himself. And it was this deep-seated grief that had ushered Julian across his dividing line. But speak of these things to his father? Impossible.

The view from the window of the aircraft showed the green striations of the Appalachian Range beneath them, the long streamers of mountains and valleys, as Julian concluded the most difficult part of his narration, ". . . I guess he took it sometime while I was asleep maybe and copied it." And then almost immediately he felt the need

to defend, and he said, "It didn't get into the paper, but
he was the one who threw the grenade out the window."

The trailing edge of the wing moving forward revealed
a small factory town by a river beneath them with black
smoke belching up from chimneys and Julian thought
again of that moment. He said, "It blew up in a field with
a big bang." But then as his thoughts turned back to the
more recent events, he murmured half to himself, "He
said he needed it more than I did." And here Julian
turned and looked at his father and again Aldrin West
was aware of change and that it was no longer a child
speaking to him when Julian said briefly and quietly, "I
guess maybe he did."

West, however, momentarily mistook it for the helplessness of the young and therefore supplied some adult
belligerence. He said, "Look here, Julian, we can fight it.
He could never win in court. I'm a witness as to when you
made it. He wouldn't dare stand up to it. We can beat
him."

Julian, once more lost in thought, was looking out of
the window again at country that had flattened out into
broken hills and the beginning of Midwestern farmlands.

But then Julian became aware that his father had
spoken to him and what he had said, and he replied
simply, "I don't want to."

Aldrin West became confused for here again was that
dark gap within his son that he did not understand, the
shell he was unable to penetrate. What shadows had
fallen upon this boy? Had something too terrible to re-
late happened to him? He felt his own guilt come choking up into his throat and he was miserably frightened

until common sense once more reasserted itself. Julian's story had been straightforward enough. He had encountered a rascal and had been taken by him. He tried another tack.

"Well, then, see, it doesn't really matter that much then, does it, Julian? What's important really is that you set out to do something and you got there and what's more you made it all by yourself. You've shown that you're a man. . . ." West had wanted to go on with this speech into even more fulsome praise such as, "By God, you've proved to me that I have a son. I'll never forget it again. I'm proud of you," but it all dried up against the barrier of Julian's absence once more.

Julian should have been glowing at this praise, filled with delight and experiencing that wonderful tickling feeling beneath the breastbone that comes when one is complimented, but he didn't. He had hardly heard the speech. His mind had been turning back to the trip and all the times that Marshall had been there when he needed him, and at times when he hadn't even known what it was all about, and he saw once more the gay, half-amused, half-mocking expression on Marshall's face.

West was saying, "That Colonel What's-His-Name— Sisson. It isn't often that a boy of your age can earn the respect of a man like that. He thought you were pretty marvelous. He told me how you just walked in right through the Pentagon Building."

The name of Sisson had Julian's attention for a moment. He thought gratefully of the Colonel's help and kindness but once more there was a mystery there and

it traced back, as did almost everything, to Marshall.
Always Marshall. Marshall running down the aisle of the
bus to the Colonel after which they had both got off in
pursuit of that other little man. And Marshall had come
back alone and hinted something about secret stuff and
spies.

Julian's memory pictures were still unreeling scenes
through his head and he suddenly laughed aloud and
when his father looked at him said, "He got the truck
driver to take us and then he changed me into Buffalo
Bill and made me pretend to shoot an Indian."

West said, "Eh?" He had not heard that bit before. He
said, "Truck driver? Indian? What was that all about?"

But Julian was away again. He said, "Oh, nothing."

West felt himself seized by the most dreadful pang of
jealousy. He was Julian's natural father. He ought to
come first with him. And yet someone else had managed
to take his place. But this was ridiculous too. The boy
had had an exciting adventure, a momentary relationship with an apparently attractive ex-soldier type who
would be a hero to any child, and then had been brutally
pushed up against his first encounter with the feet of
clay. Goddammit, he loved his son. He wanted to throw
his arms about the thin shoulders of this boy and hold
him hard to himself and shelter him. Instead he felt
himself pushed into flat, meaningless sentences such as
"There's the Mississippi down there. Old Man River."

The broad, winding yellow snake crawling across the
face of the map was below them. Julian said, "I know. We
came over it on a bridge. Marshall said he went down it
on a riverboat once . . ."

A little later something which had been at the back of Aldrin's head ever since he had become reunited with his son surfaced into an exclamation of surprise. "Hey! what happened to your stammer, Julian?"

Julian, without even looking up at him, replied, "Aw, who needs it? Marshall said to cut it out."

The plane was over the Rockies and West observed, "The Great Divide."

Julian said, "Uh huh. Marshall said if you poured a glass of water over it half would go into the Pacific and the other half into the Atlantic. We went over the pass and there was a man who played a funny instrument. I wonder what happened to him?"

West regarded his son with a sense of total helplessness. He knew he hadn't been getting through to him at all. But he had yet one more card to play. They would be arriving home soon. Would they then fall back into their old ways and would he and his son be separate and unhappy? He played his card.

"I'll tell you what we could do. You know down below next to the trunk room which is sort of half storage and we don't use? We could make it a kind of lab there. I mean, not a lab, but a place where, you know, you can work out any ideas you have. We could fix up a lathe or anything you need. A drawing board and things like that."

At this Julian looked at his father. He nodded a slow and reflective assent but said nothing and returned with his attention riveted to the window and the world below which had now become the wild moonscape of the badlands of the West, the bluffs, canyons and escarpments, the tumbled country akin to that which carried the deepest memories for Julian.

And looking down from thirty thousand feet Julian actually espied, reduced to an almost microscopic insect, a bus crawling along on a lonely stretch of road and in a moment it seemed that he was transported there again onto old 396 sitting next to Marshall and munching on a hamburger, moistening it with Coke. The whine of the tires was in his ears mingled with the music of the hurdy-gurdy. He saw the faces of the chess players again and Marge and Bill leaning towards one another always as though magnetized, their fingers intertwined. And then there had been that trip from Albuquerque and those two funny sisters and all the different friendly people and he was both amongst them below and up in the airplane as well watching the bus crawl around a curve.

". . . and we could work it out together."

His father's voice broke in upon Julian's vision. Apparently he had been continuing talking all the time that Julian had made his little voyage to earth. Julian was then again back in the aircraft, and turning from the window he gave his father a half smile and said, "Okay, thanks. That would be great."

Aldrin had expected more enthusiasm or perhaps even some kind of physical contact from his son. They had yet to touch one another since their meeting. Julian hadn't even taken his proffered hand when they had made their way through the airport in Washington. To cover his disappointment he now himself looked down out of the window over Julian's shoulder. The landscape had changed again.

West said, "We ought to be home in about an hour now. Your mother will be so happy."

Julian made no reply.

There was no doubt but that Julian had changed and grown up. The manifestations were subtle, a slight difference in the way he wore his clothes, even the sound of his footsteps, and yet he remained remote and locked in and it was quite possible that this enabled him to survive the spate of publicity that had attended his return. In some manner Julian managed to give the impression that all that was being written, printed and talked about with regard to the adventure had to do with somebody else and not himself. He was able to remain aloof from it all.

His father tried daily. He tried hard. His eyes had actually been opened to the gap which had existed between himself and his son and to the insensitivity of his own behavior. He had been badly frightened by Julian's escapade, which might have ended in total disaster. His problem was that he did not know what to do. He was too long laced into the straitjacket of adult ways of thinking and acting and he did not know how to extricate himself. His avenues of approach to Julian consisted of showing an exaggerated interest in his extracurricular activities and Julian accepted this gratefully and responded to his father's show of concern. Yet Aldrin West was aware that he never achieved any genuine closeness or penetration of this curious reserve which had fallen upon the boy ever since he had found him in Washington.

West did not know of one major achievement on his

part, which was that by all the evidence of his concern over Julian's trip, and above all by his crossing the continent to bring Julian home, he had shown him that he cared and had restored some of his son's trust in him. As with many children, Julian's feelings about his father had been based partly upon fact, partly upon fantasies, and the latter were now dispelled. And the relationship between father and son would have returned to a more normal everyday one except that West had no way of knowing the depth of the trauma that Julian had suffered on a totally different level.

West was a businessman and not a psychiatrist or even a person with too much understanding, or he might have thought it strange that Julian had never broken down. One would have expected a child of his age to shed tears at being robbed of the most important thing he had ever achieved, a creation all his own. West, during the ensuing days, was often to wonder at Julian's stony-faced acceptance of things as they were. Outwardly he was a normal schoolboy. The laboratory built in the basement had to be accounted a huge success, for when his homework was done Julian was always down there tinkering and working. But once the excitement over the adventure had subsided Julian never referred to it again and the curious barrier between his father and himself stayed. As for his mother, she remained blissfully unaware. She had her son back. She was pleased with her husband's efforts and the minor manifestations of Julian's independence were realized without too much regret. After all, one had to accept the fact that one's children did grow up. What was satisfactory was that her husband had had a lesson and appeared to have profited by it.

It was thus several months later that Julian came home from school, entering the vestibule noisily, dropping his satchel on the floor, slinging his cap accurately up onto one of the hooks of the hatrack, and heard his mother's voice from abovestairs.

"That you, Julian?"

"Yeah, Mom."

"How was school?"

"Fine. I'm going down to my shop, Mom."

"Don't you want a glass of milk, Julian?"

"No thanks, not now."

Here was an example, a small one albeit, of Julian's newly won status. Before, his mother would have insisted upon his having the glass of milk and would have had it slightly warmed since cold milk on the stomach was supposed to be bad. Now there was no further attempt at persuasion, only the usual query, "Have you any homework?"

Julian replied, "Not much. I'll do it downstairs." He slung his satchel again over his shoulder and went down the cellar steps. He hurried through his lessons and thereafter became engrossed in a mechanical problem that he had not solved.

Due to his youth and inexperience Julian's mechanical bent was still imitative and adaptive like his transformation of a water pistol into a Bubble Gun. Now he was working on a flight toy he had acquired, a disk which consisted of four blades with a spring in the central hub. When the spring was pressed down by means of a stick,

it caused the disk to spin rapidly and, due to the pitch of
the blades, rise vertically from the ground in a short
flight. Julian's idea was to convert this into a helicopter
toy. He had made several drawings and even one mock-
up, but the activation of the blades was still a difficulty.

But he was happy enough with his long workbench
equipped with a lathe, electric drill and a vise. There
were drawers and receptacles for materials such as sheets
of tin, bits of plywood, nails and screws, and his tools
were neatly contained in a rack. He had also been provided with a special drawing-board table and the necessary implements.

One of the best things about the place was its alone-
ness. His mother never came down; it was understood
that he was to keep it clean himself, and did, and there
with the cellar door closed and lights blazing and the
stillness except for the occasional whine of his drill, it
was as though he were wearing yet another skin, a second
Julian. And sometimes while that second was functioning, the first one, he himself, the inside Julian, would fall
into a reverie. His thoughts would wander far afield from
where he was and what he was doing and old sadnesses
would be revived.

At six Aldrin West came home, set his briefcase down
and looked casually through the letters on the salver on
the side table, the late afternoon delivery. One of them
brought a look of curiosity to his face and he examined
both sides of it without learning much. He called out,
"Julian?"

The reply came from below, "I'm down here, Dad."

With the puzzling letter in his hand West descended the steps into Julian's workshop and asked, "Who do you know in Sheridan, Alabama, Julian?"

Julian looked up from the bit of tin he had locked in his vise for shaping and asked, "Where?"

His father repeated, "Sheridan, Alabama," and handed him the letter. "It's addressed to you."

Julian took it and examined it: "Julian West, 137 East View Terrace, San Diego, California," in a style of wandering handwriting that gave him a strange and creepy feeling, as though the envelope itself communicated something to his fingertips, or had absorbed some kind of message and sent it along down to his stomach. He stood there holding it and looking at it until his father said, "Well, why don't you open it and find out."

Julian picked up the screwdriver from his workbench, slit the envelope and removed the letter therefrom, and his father, looking over his shoulder, saw that it was written on the letterhead of Collins Garage, 43 Main Street, Sheridan, Alabama. Directly beneath this had been pasted a cutting from a cheap magazine. It was an advertisement from a mail-order-house toy company for an article that looked very much like the one Julian had invented. It was a one-column, two-inch-square ad with the picture of a gun with soap bubbles emerging from the muzzle. The text boasted:

> **Bubblegat! Looks like the real thing. But shoots bubbles. Amaze your friends. Every boy should have a Bubblegat. Order now while they last. Fill out**

the coupon and send $1.65 to
include the cost of mailing to
Bubblegat, P.O. Box 37, Fort
Lauderdale, Florida.

The man and the boy stared at this advertisement for a moment uncomprehending, then their attention was drawn to the handwritten scrawl beneath it.

West asked, "What does it say?"

Julian read out loud carefully and meticulously since there was some difficulty with the handwriting.

> *"Dear Julian, Ha-ha. I guess this will give you a big laugh. I was a boob, but it shows you are a real inventor and had a great idea only somebody beat us to it. So I was a rat for nothing. Like I said I blew all my dough so I am down here in Sheridan working in a garage. Hope you are OK. Your old pal, Frank Marshall."*

Julian finished reading, and as he had reached the end his chin and lower lip had begun to tremble and his face had screwed up curiously. He placed the letter on his workbench, tears already streaming from his eyes, put his face down on his arms and gave way to crying. For the first time since the disaster in Washington, the emotional dam had burst, his weeping was the drawing out of the agony which had so long lived in his heart.

Aldrin West looked at his son with amazement and said, "C'mon, son, what are you crying about? It serves him damn well right. He asked for it and he got it."

Julian raised his head from his arms only long enough to shake his head in negation before he was seized by a fresh paroxysm of sobs.

His father groped, "Is it because somebody else

thought of the Bubble Gun first? Look, it can happen to anyone. It shows you your invention was okay."

Punctuated by sobs and half smothered because the small head was still buried in his arms came the words, "Who cares about an old Bubble Gun."

West was still alarmed and bewildered by the sudden breakdown of his son, so unexpected and, too, so frightening, in that somewhere buried in the back of his mind was the thought that it was not quite the reaction that one would expect from a child.

He asked, "Then what are you crying about?"

The muffled reply emerged from the buried head, "Marshall."

West picked up the letter and read through it again and for the first time had one of those moments of clarity that are able to sweep away differences, stupidities, blockages and blindness and demolish all barriers between two humans. He let the letter fall back upon the workbench and put a comforting arm about Julian's shoulder. He said, "Julian. I guess perhaps I understand. We'll write to him. Maybe we can give him a hand."

Julian lifted his head from his arms and looked up at his father who was standing close beside him. He looked at him and through him and in his ears rang the simple phrase that West had used in all sincerity, "Maybe we can give him a hand." Julian put his arms about his father's waist and his face against the rough pocket of his jacket and hugged him hard.